Book One of *THE MIDDLE WORLD*

Your book was excellent!!! I loved it so much and I know a lot of people between the ages of 6th and 9th grade would for sure agree!!! You are such a phenomenal writer and really did such an amazing job bringing all the characters to life!! Thank you for letting me read your magical book!! I'm so honored!! It is going to be such a huge success!!
    – **LILY KRAFT**, *student at the*
Colorado Rocky Mountain School in Carbondale, Colorado

Thanks for letting [Darrell and me] read your manuscript. It is an imaginative, intriguing and interesting tale that provides historical information as well as provocative thoughts about spiritual matters...You have some wonderful descriptive passages, and the children and their lives as depicted bring lots of issues to light!
    – **JANE MUNSELL**, *tour guide at the Redstone Castle and*
editor for/wife of **DARRELL MUNSELL, PhD**, *Professor Emeritus,*
West Texas A&M University and author of "From Redstone to Ludlow: John
Cleveland Osgood's Struggle against the United Mine Workers of America"

The Middle World is at once a vibrant introduction to the beauty of the Crystal River Valley, a riveting adventure into the spirit realm, a developmentally appropriate coming-of-age story for juveniles and adults alike, and a much-needed reminder about the importance of inter-generational reconciliation in keeping our world coherent and whole.
    – **ADRIAN FIELDER, PhD** *(Comparative Literature,*
Northwestern University), children's literacy expert, Professor and
Assistant Dean of Instruction at Colorado Mountain College

This enchanting story will delight young readers, introducing them to the tenets of spirituality as they follow adventurous Rose and Kenai on their journey through Redstone, Colorado's storied past. *The Middle World* champions the magic and wonder of both the natural and supernatural world, urging us to put down our digital devices in search for greater meaning, connection and purpose. I, for one, fell in love with its curious and lovable characters, finding myself more and more drawn into their discoveries. An absolute pleasure!
    – **DANIELLE BEINSTEIN, MA** *(Spiritual Psychology,*
University of Santa Monica), astrologist and spiritual advisor,
meditation guide at Unplug.

Conchiss Publications

 CONCHISS

Although *The Middle World* is inspired by some real people and historical events, the story is a work of fiction.

www.themiddleworld.com

ISBN #9781517771850

July 2016

THE MIDDLE WORLD

BOOK ONE

by

Nicole Beinstein

Illustrations by

Brittany Kohari

Handwritten inscription: Dear Emma, May the spirit of Redstone bless you always. Enjoy the story! With love, N

for my parents, who gave me life

for my children and their father, who saved it

and for the memory

of my beloved Aunt Judy

who always believed

I thought then

of the collective memory of the land,

of the ways in which

people and animals

and geological events

cannot help but leave scars,

sculpt wonders,

and weave stories

onto its cover.

Alexandra Fuller

Leaving Before the Rains Come (2015)

Hotel Colorado

I-70

Glenwood Springs

82

Carbondale

Roaring Fork

133

Crystal River

Coal Creek

Coal Creek Rd.

General Store

Coke Ovens

Redstone

Redstone Castle

CRYSTAL RIVER VALLEY

Marble

B. Kohari 2013

Part 1: Rose

1

*R*ose let the screen door slam shut, and even stayed on the front stoop for a minute to wait for her mother's response. But, as usual, her mother said nothing, not even an okay, as she sat in front of her television set eating potato chips and sipping cold coffee from an old SkiCorp Lift Operations mug.

"I'll be back before sundown," Rose yelled through the screen before shutting the splintered and lavender paint-chipped front door.

Rose hopped on her turquoise bike and headed down the boulevard. As she pedaled along the fast-flowing river, she turned her head for a few magpies flying by, and caught a glimpse of a deer or elk prancing through the trees. The aspen leaves were shaking in the breeze. The smells of juniper filled the air with summer sweetness.

She reached the end of the road, across from the twin camp-sites, and set her bike down on the reddish dirt. She walked down to the river. She had never been to an ocean before, so this was the closest she ever got to a beach; albeit this one was only about fifty feet from the river (give or take, depending on the season), scattered with various colored and sized rocks, but mostly dark grey. The sand was more like the thick, blackish clay from a ceramics class than the white sand that pours down an hourglass.

Finding a happy family playing in the water and wading on the slippery stones, she headed downstream, behind the enor-mous maroon boulder to a secret nook she thought no one but she knew about. It was her spot. And she could spend hours there, dreaming about traveling the world, singing, and making a big name for herself.

On this particular afternoon she was singing a song about rainbows. She loved that song; it was from an old movie about a frog puppet that plays his guitar on a log in the middle of a swamp, fantasizing about becoming famous, and yet comfort-able just where he is. And then, out of nowhere in this movie, paddles up a man who calls himself an agent, and asks the frog if he wants to be a star in Hollywood, handing the frog his busi-ness card like a magic trick. Is that how it happens? she asked herself. When something is meant to be does it just row its boat right in front of your face and give you a card?

At the very moment when the vision of the movie escaped her mind, she spotted a man with a black bowler hat wearing dirty corduroys, pant-legs rolled at the ankle, and a white button-down shirt. He was sitting on a chunk of pebbles, staring at her, as if expecting her to be the first one to talk. She turned her body quickly to the left then took a second look back at him. He continued to sit there, his eyes piercing hers.

Rose thought the man had a soft and gentle face; a kind and knowing face that gave her curiosity more weight than her fear. There was something strangely familiar about him, as if she'd met him some place else before, though she couldn't conjure up the place or time in her memory.

"Hello," she yelled across the river.

And then he was gone.

She closed her eyes for a second, pressed her hands against her face, but upon releasing them, she felt a presence beside her.

"Hello," he said, almost in a whisper.

"How…how…?" she stammered, moving her body a foot or so away from him.

"It's okay. I just wanted to make sure you could really see me," he said.

"Of course I can see you. Why wouldn't I be able to see you?" she asked.

"A lot of people can't," he answered.

She didn't really know what he meant by that. Did he mean that no one could really see who he was inside, the same way she felt about herself?

"I have to go now," he said. "But can we meet here another time?"

"I guess so," she said. She knew never to talk to a strange man, and yet this young man seemed harmless, completely and utterly harmless. Before she could even finish her thought, though, he disappeared again.

"Wait!" she shouted. "Wait…when?"

Silence.

She sat by the river for a long time after that, trying hard to make sense of the strange man's sudden appearance, and sudden disappearance. She couldn't figure out why she wasn't afraid, or why she couldn't cry about it, or even why the man had chosen her of all people to speak to, although it was true there had been no one else in that space besides them.

But even if she always believed she was special somehow, she didn't want it to be in this way. Not special in a way that made her weird, but special in the opposite way, special in a way that would make her feel universally accepted, that would make her popular.

Maybe this man wasn't real, she capitulated, a figment of her imagination, or perhaps he was from another world, but she couldn't give those ideas too much room to grow, at least not yet. She recalled the time she sat in bed, contemplating the universe: she let her imagination take her into outer space, heading toward infinity, far, far, away into an endless nothingness, and then she stopped, too scared to let her imagination push any further into the deep dark void. So just like then, she blocked her thought process dead in its tracks, stood up, and left.

She climbed back up the trail to her bike, headed for home. She pedaled as fast as she could, fully focused on the road, on her heartbeat, on the burning sensation in her legs.

As she approached her cream and violet-outlined Victorian house with the dilapidated white picket fence, she sped ahead. It was too early. She didn't want to go home just yet. She had already finished her library book, and the last thing she wanted to do was watch TV with her mom. Her dad was gone for the day. Working, even though it was a weekend.

So Rose pedaled on by, past the General Store on the left and the playground on the right, past the Inn towards the road along the river leading to the castle. She parked her bike before the dirt road, and started walking the path. As she neared the hill she stepped back, thinking she had heard something move in the woods. She waited a moment. When she decided it was nothing, she slowly turned around and walked back to her bike. She didn't know what to do with herself, or where to go. She settled on the playground, and ended up chatting with a family who was staying at the campground as part of their summer vacation.

As the sun set behind the giant red cliffs, Rose said goodbye to the friendly family as they headed back to their campground. Thinking she was alone, she turned towards the swings only to find Kenai already swinging.

Rose froze, almost star-struck, until an invisible force pulled her towards the adjacent swing, stripping away any power her father's words held over her.

When she walked around the steel bars and moved backwards into the rubber-seated swing, Kenai noticed her.

"Oh, hi," he said. "I didn't even know you were there!"

"I'm sorry. Did I frighten you?" she asked.

"No," he laughed. "Not at all."

They both started swinging in unison, until Kenai swung especially high and jumped off onto the wood-chipped ground below. She copied him, her heart leaping out of her chest whenever she landed. They did this over and over again, until they left the swings to chase each other across the burgundy steel bridge. After a couple of amicable races back and forth over the bridge, they retreated to the riverbank and settled into chucking rocks into the water.

When they finally calmed down from all their movement, they began to talk.

"How do you like your school?" she asked him.

"I love it," he said. "I love all the outdoor adventures we go on, and the teachers are really nice. Especially the music teacher."

"You like music?"

"Love it," he said. "I play the piano."

"You do? For how long?"

"Since I was five," he answered.

"Was it hard to learn?"

"Not really. And it's pretty easy now. For the most part."

"I wish I could play an instrument," she said, crushing some softened shale under her foot.

"So, why don't you?"

"Can't afford it," she said. "But I like to sing, and that's free."

"Maybe I could teach you? You know, to play the piano?" he suggested, skipping a smooth slate rock into the water.

She thought about his offer for a minute, and so badly wanted to say yes. But she knew that would never happen.

Kenai was a tall, handsome boy, with liquid brown eyes. He possessed the most natural smile she'd ever seen. If only they went to the same school, they could be friends. Her dad wouldn't be able to do anything about it then. But here, on the boulevard, everyone knew each other, and talked, and her dad would find out soon enough if the two of them were hanging out together a lot.

In any case, Rose was going to enjoy this perfect moment she had with Kenai. She wasn't going to let bad thoughts about her dad get in the way of the special time she and Kenai were having together.

"Would you rather play the guitar?" Kenai questioned Rose when she didn't respond to him.

"Oh, I guess," she said quickly, praying that he couldn't read her mind. "It would be easier to travel and sing with than a piano. I'd like to write my own songs one day."

6

"Me, too!" he exclaimed. "I've actually written a few already, but they're not very good."

"Oh, I'm sure they are! Can you sing one for me now?"

"No way," he blushed, and threw a perforated basalt rock across the river.

"I'm sorry," she said, shuffling a handful of sandstone rocks between her hands. "I didn't mean to-"

"It's fine," he replied. "I'm just kind of embarrassed about that sort of thing, you know, when I'm put on the spot."

"I'm the same way," she said.

They stood there by the river, speechless and motionless for what felt like an eternity. They watched an eagle soar above them, and a squirrel scurry up a pine tree. A cool wind passed between them. They looked to the sky and observed a large, grey cloud as it concealed the blinding sun.

"Guess it's time to go," Rose said, releasing her pebbles onto the ground.

"Guess so," Kenai agreed.

They strolled back over the bridge to the sounds of toddlers giggling on the twisty slide.

"Wanna get a piece of candy?" she suggested, pointing to the Redstone General Store across the street.

"No, thanks," he said. "I'm not really supposed to have candy."

"Oh," she said under her breath.

They followed one another down the boulevard until they reached Kenai's home. The olive green house had a hanging bench suspended above a large deck that wrapped around the front. There were planted flowers leading to the house and several wheeled toys on the grass.

"What does Kenai mean?" she found the courage to ask him

at the end of their walk.

"Black bear. It's a place in Alaska. My parents went there on their honeymoon."

"Cool," she said.

"My little sister's name is Desta, which means 'happiness,'" he replied. "It's an East African name. They already picked out my name before they decided to adopt me, so only my middle name is African. Bekele. It means 'grown up,' or something like that. It's actually the name my birth parents gave me," he said, speaking quickly towards the end of his description.

"Kenai Bekele," she pronounced aloud. "What a beautiful name."

"Thanks," he said, looking into her grey-blue, almond-shaped eyes. "So's Rose."

"Rose Sonoma," she clarified.

"Oh, wow. Even prettier," he said with a large grin, and then looked to the ground.

"Okay, well…" she replied, starting to walk away in case he invited her into his house.

"Okay. See you later," he uttered.

"Later," she repeated, already a few steps down the road.

When she made it back to her house, she opened the front door and shouted, "I'm home," then fixed herself some cereal for dinner, finishing the crossword puzzle her mom had started that morning.

She undressed in her bedroom and skipped into the bathroom wearing the fluorescent jellybean robe her Grandma YaYa sent her last Christmas. She turned on the shower with the rusted faucets. She stepped into the aquamarine tiled stall, moldy brown in the corners, singing an old romantic song about holding hands softly to herself.

"You've been in there long enough, Rosie! You need to save some hot water for your dad! He'll be home any minute," her mom yelled.

Rose promptly got out of the shower, dried herself off, brushed her teeth, put on her favorite pair of green monkey pajamas, and warmed up under the bed covers. She started rereading her library book about a mysterious tollbooth, hoping it would put her to sleep before the end of the first chapter.

By the time she reached the third page, her dad had come home. He opened her bedroom door and asked, "You still up, pumpkin?" His growing beard was stubbly, highlighting his already pronounced cheekbones. He was wearing his signature red baseball cap, his thick, strawberry blonde hair nearly touching his shoulders. He was more handsome than any movie star Rose had ever seen in pictures.

"Yeah," she whispered back.

"Why you whispering?" he asked as he neared her bed.

"Don't know really....how was work?" she asked him.

"Okay, just fixing up some stuff at a restaurant."

"Ella's?"

"Yeah, Ella's...Well, I just wanted to say goodnight," he said, and then kissed her on the cheek. She sat up to hug him. He hugged her back tightly.

"I love you, Daddy."

"I love you, too, pumpkin," he said in his slight Southern accent, kissing her other cheek. "Get some sleep now," he instructed.

"I will," she promised as he turned off her bedside lamp and walked into the adjacent bathroom. She could hear the shower start; the noise from the water calmed her into a peaceful slumber, quieting her anxious thoughts about the man at the river and her afternoon with Kenai.

2

*F*irst thing next morning Rose biked down to her same spot on the river. Along the road, she ran into her pet fox, Mechau, whom she had named after a well-known artist who once lived in Redstone with his wife and four children.

She stopped in the road, several steps before Mechau.

"You love me, don't you, Mechau?" she asked him.

The fox moved his body ever so slightly.

"I love you, too, Mechau. You know I do, right?"

The fox yawned then scratched his body with his left hind leg.

"Because it feels really good to love someone, and to tell them you love them, right?" she said. He stretched again, and she got back on her bike, pedaling even faster than before.

Mechau followed Rose to her favorite spot on the river, the

"stage" as she referred to it in her mind. He scooted close to her once Rose was off her bike again. When they both reached the giant boulder together and Rose sat down, he curled his body, resting several feet to the right of her.

She began to sing another rainbow song when her mysterious friend appeared, now several feet away from her, to her left.

This time she addressed him immediately.

"Hi," she said, twisting her body both away and closer to him at the same time; it was an awkward, acrobatic move, with one shoulder nearer to him, and the other shoulder further away.

"Hi," he said. He was wearing the same old-fashioned outfit as before, but his hat looked a little messier. The hairs on Mechau's back quickly stood up, and he scurried away through the boulders. Rose reached out for Mechau, but then let the idea of chasing him go, more intrigued by her new friend.

"Do you live around here?" she asked delicately.

"Yes," he said. "For a while now."

"I live here, too," she said. "On the boulevard."

"Which house?" he asked coyly.

"The cream and purple one, a few houses up from the cafe." She immediately worried that maybe she shouldn't have told him as much, but then let the thought go.

"The Wright house?" he asked.

"I don't know of any Wrights," she said. "Did they live here a long time ago? Because we've been in our house almost nine years now; I moved in when I was three and a half."

"Time doesn't mean much to me," he said in a weepy sort of voice.

"What does that mean?" she asked him.

"*Difficile* to explain," he said. "Kind of like it doesn't exist." His eyes appeared more distant, as if he were in another world already.

"Oh," she said softly. "What's your name?"

"Manuele," he answered.

"Like 'ukelele,'" she giggled unexpectedly.

"Somewhat, I suppose," he said. "My little sister called me Manu, though."

"That's so cute!" Rose exclaimed.

"Would you rather call me Manu?" he asked.

"If you don't mind," she answered elatedly.

"Okay, then you will call me Manu, *bellissima.*"

"Thank you," she said, smiling. "How old are you?"

"Twenty-five, I think," he said.

"You don't know?" she questioned him.

"Twenty-five when I died," he replied curtly. "Not sure what that makes me today, whatever day today is."

"I don't understand," she said, her voice high-pitched, at which point Manu disappeared into thin air.

Rose turned around in a full circle, hoping that somehow that would make him reappear so he could explain himself better. A chill ran through her entire body.

She ran to her bike, and this time she pedaled as hard as she possibly could, past the firehouse, past the back entrance to town, past her home, past the cafe, the General Store, the park, antique store, church, art center, and the Redstone Inn, to the front entrance of the town, across the two-lane highway (against her parents' rules because cars and large trucks often went as fast as seventy miles per hour on it), a few yards past the restored coke ovens towards Coal Basin along Coal Creek, where she biked even harder up the long and winding road.

Over one hundred years ago Redstone and its sister town Coal

Basin together were a fully functioning coal-mining village owned by the Colorado Fuel and Iron Company. Coal Basin was situated twelve miles northwest of the highway, where once a train, the Crystal River Railroad, ran through with designated stops along the way to carry people and transport coke, another form of coal. The actual coal mining took place in Coal Basin, which employed approximately two hundred sixty-five American, Austrian and Italian men. After the coal was transported down the treacherous High Line stretch of the railway to the highway, it cooked in rows of two hundred beehive ovens until it became coke over a period of two to three days. At their peak these round ovens, made of stone and covered with hardened brown dirt, were producing over six million tons of coke per year.

Turning the coal into coke, which resembled brownish moonrocks instead of the amorphous quality of raw coal's gritty black sand, allowed for an even higher-quality fuel than coal. The trains would then transport the coke all over the country to heat buildings and homes, but also to use at steel-making factories.

Coke smelts iron from its core, creating steel that can be used for industrial construction. During the middle to late 1800s, America was growing at a fierce rate, due in large part to all the newly available energy (coal, oil and gas), and the strong materials and technology made possible by the new energy. It was an energy boom like the pending one, Rose had learned at school.

The town of Redstone, a stone's throw on the other side of the highway, was where the owner of the Colorado Fuel and Iron Company lived a century ago. Redstone had never completely shut down, whereas Coal Basin had long been abandoned and its many buildings (including seventy cottages, a school, company store, and clubhouse) destroyed.

⊚ ⊚ ⊚

Rose made it as far up Coal Creek Road as the camping area, huffing and puffing, desperately trying to catch her breath. She sat down on the tiny bridge, hanging her legs over the side, watching the creek scurry downhill, and cried. She cried harder and harder until she could hardly breathe.

Eventually she took some long, full breaths. In through the nose. Out through the mouth. Over and over again. Breathe in. Breathe out.

It *is* possible that ghosts exist, she reminded herself. It is possible.

She wasn't sure how long she'd been sitting on the side of the road, maybe she was losing a sense of time herself, but she was getting hungry and ready for lunch. She analyzed over and over what she should do about Manu, how she should think about him, if she ever wanted to see him again, if she'd force herself to forget the whole thing, if that was even possible, thinking, thinking, thinking, until her mind turned to mush, and she couldn't think clearly anymore.

Letting go of her over-analytical mind allowed her heart to speak louder, which suggested she find a way to remain sane, but also to figure out the truth. Finally calm, she hopped back on her bike and let the downhill take over her ride. The wind rushed past her as if they were in a race together. She biked across the highway to the boulevard, past the Redstone Church with its vibrant stained-glass windows. She looked up at the church's ironclad bell just as it rang out for noon.

She sped by Kenai who was spinning on the tire swing, but averted his eyes.

Peanut butter and banana sandwich with a glass of milk and a side of raw carrots - that's what she craved for lunch.

As she sat down at the kitchen table with her sandwich, Rose spotted Mechau outside of the cracked window. She went to the front porch, where he met her.

"It's okay, Mechau," she said to him. "There's nothing to be afraid of. Manu just needs a friend, and we can be his friend."

She knelt down and petted Mechau, and for the first time he didn't dash away; he let her touch him and rub his orange-furred back and ears.

"Thank you, Mechau," Rose said with a giant smile across her tear-stained face.

Rose's mom turned into the driveway suddenly. Mechau took off then, just before Susie exited her green Subaru.

"Give me a hand, will ya?" Susie called to Rose.

Rose carried the plastic grocery bags to the door.

"Why didn't you use the cloth bags, Mom?"

"Who can remember to always bring them from the house to the car and then to the store? That's way too much work. And anyway, I like using the plastic ones for the garbage cans in the bathroom."

"But it's better for the environment to use the cloth ones," Rose argued.

"Is that the crap they teach you in school these days?" her mom said. "It doesn't make one bit of difference, Rosie. What a waste of time to be teaching you that crap."

"But, Mom- " Rose tried to finish her sentence while they were both setting the bags on the kitchen island.

"What, Rose? Enough!" was all her mom could say.

"Soon you won't even be able to get plastic bags at the store," Rose finished quickly. "You'll have to bring your own."

"What're you talking about?"

"They passed a law. I thought you knew. It's been in all the papers," Rose said.

"In the papers, huh? The local papers? You know I don't read those. Who cares what happens in this boring, stupid place, anyway?"

It was just another one of those tough days, Rose thought. There were more of these days for her mom lately, and less and less of her mom's good days. Rose felt powerless to do anything about it; the best she could do, she realized, was to not let her mom's bad moods crawl inside of her, no matter how impossible that seemed at times.

Rose moved away from the conversation and brought in the Chicago daily newspaper wrapped in blue plastic from the mailbox and placed it on the kitchen island. Susie, that was her mom's name, followed all the current news from Chicago. The epicenter of the world existed in Chicago. But there really was nothing left there for Susie, except for a couple of long lost friends whom she hadn't spoken to in years. Her parents had both passed away and her sisters had all settled in separate parts of California. Susie hadn't lived in Chicago for over twenty years already, and she actually had left the city in a mad rush, to escape the overpopulation, the cars, the traffic, the smog, the rat race. At first she loved the mountains, the clean air, the open space, the freedom, where she could breathe deeply. But now she felt suffocated by the expanse.

Her mom leafed through the paper with her freshly manicured hands. Pale pink nail polish, as always.

"Monica's parents are getting divorced," her mom announced, moving the newspaper out of her sight.

"Really?" Rose asked.

"Really, Rosie," her mom said in an odd sort of way.

"Why?"

"I don't know. Something about her dad working too hard."

"Oh," Rose sighed. "Do you think Daddy works too hard?"

Her mom laughed, "I wish."

"Do you think you two will ever get divorced?" Rosie asked bluntly.

"I don't know," her mom admitted. "How can someone ever know something like that until it actually happens?"

"I don't know," Rose sighed.

As Rose walked towards her orange-striped bedroom, her mom shouted, "What're you doing?"

"I'm changing," Rose yelled back.

"For what?" Susie shouted, slamming the cabinet and refrigerator doors closed. Susie was very loud whenever she was doing chores in the house; she was no Mary Poppins, as Joe, her husband and Rose's dad, often reminded her. Joe had learned how to clean and keep things in order as a military officer, and Susie could never live up to his meticulous standards.

"It's Wednesday night. Family swim night at the Inn," Rose yelled out. After a few moments she added, "Don't worry, it's free, remember?"

"Oh, okay," Susie said.

Rose put on her favorite two-piece (a black, pink and purple zebra-printed bathing suit) then tossed on her magenta-sprinkled summer dress, slipped into yellow flip-flops, threw a ragged white beach towel into her backpack, and ran out the front door without saying goodbye.

"Bye, Rosie," her mom said from the couch in front of the television set. But it was too late for Rose to hear her; she was already on her bike and on her way.

Rose arrived at the Inn before it got too crowded. She saved a lounge chair with her monogrammed backpack (a birthday present from one of her aunts) and jumped into the pool. Rose was supposed to be there with an adult because there wasn't a lifeguard on duty, but she clung onto one or another family close enough so that no one noticed just how alone she actually was.

Rose felt like a dolphin when she swam, diving down to the bottom of the water, pushing herself back up to catch some air at the surface, and then diving down again, arching and curving her back in line with her steady head, gliding as much as she could glide in an overpopulated pool.

She swam until the sun was far behind the giant red cliffs that protected the Crystal Valley. As soon as the sun went down, the air temperature dropped at least fifteen degrees.

Rose intermittently looked around for Kenai. It seemed like half the town was at the pool that day, indulging in the three-dollar hot dogs and five-dollar hamburgers (potato chips included), cannonball-jumping into the deep-end, parents circling around their babies in inner tubes, cold bodies heating up in the sauna several feet away from the pool.

Rose swam until she was almost the last one remaining in the pool. She dried off quickly and walked around the back of the Inn to her bike that was laying flat to the side of one of the guest's cars, a grey Toyota Highlander with a white and blue California license plate. She was always looking for personal clues in letters and numbers, especially when she was out in public; it was just something she did to make sense of her world and to remind her that she was never truly alone. And on the Highlander's license plate she noticed the last two blue letters immediately, "KB," Kenai's initials, followed by the number "12," which was how old they both were.

3

*I*t was a warm and breezy day, and everyone was getting ready for the Fourth of July Parade. Redstone was completely full, not a single place to park on the boulevard, mostly because it was all blocked off to normal traffic; visiting cars and trucks lined up along Highway 133, north and south of the entrance to town.

Just before noon Rose rode her decorated bike to the beginning of the line, on the knoll at the base of the Redstone Inn, and greeted the familiar faces. She was wearing a Chicago baseball cap, also decorated with red and blue streamers. A nice older lady that she kind of recognized painted Rose's left cheek with a red, white and blue rainbow.

The fire truck sounded its alarm and the parade began. A

clown on stilts, then cowboys and horses followed. Local businesses strutted their big, outfitted trucks, while old-timers reminisced about the past. Those walking in the parade threw candy, while the bystanders waved to them. The elders sold pies for the community fundraising pie contest.

Rose overheard the walkers talk among themselves about their aging parents, how the weekend crowds weren't as robust as they had hoped, about the drought and the fire danger, about the barbecues and the sold-out show at the local cafe scheduled for that night.

Rose slowed down by the Redstone Museum, a one-room log house built over a century ago.

Towards the end of the parade, she saw Kenai's mom, dad and sister gathered in front of their house, spinning party favors, and blowing star-shaped whistles. But no sign of Kenai. She looked ahead of her, and behind her, searching for him, wondering how she could have missed him earlier. He quickly sped passed her, his family yelling from their house, "Go Kenai!" with large grins plastered on their faces. She had tried to catch up with him, but then saw her dad on their front porch, and waved up to him. "That's my girl," her dad said, and kicked back and forth on the rocking chair, a bottle of beer gripped in his palm. He was wearing the same faded Marine Corps sweatshirt he wore every American holiday.

"Hi, Dad," she yelled back to him, and pedaled forward in a more steady pace. She was soon at the end of the parade, and abruptly turned around, taking her time to walk her bike back to the beginning of the road.

The crowd fizzled down as she scurried around the playground. She got herself a mint chocolate chip ice cream cone from the Redstone General Store, and finished it down by the river. The wind was blowing a little stronger now, but the sun still warmed her reddish skin. She watched an Australian Shepherd puppy drink from the river, and a young family from out of town talk about what a perfect day it was, and how lucky they were to have found this parade.

"This place is like Paradise," the father commented to the mother.

"It really is," she said wistfully. "Can't imagine what it would be like to live here," the father said aloud.

"Oh, I know," the mother responded, as if they had already shared a long discussion about it, and had concluded that it would be ideal to raise their children here, but completely implausible. Well, that was usually how these kind of conversations went whenever Rose participated in them.

When Rose licked the very last drop of the ice cream and gobbled up the rest of the cone, she made her way to the Inn. She didn't want to be any part of the water hose event that the fire station sponsored every year; she was too old for that now and was in no mood to get dressed up in a hot fireman's suit and get sprayed down with water. So she sneaked in through the back by the pool, and headed down to the basement area, where a pool table, a dartboard, photos of bull riders, and a dormant TV and fireplace filled the dark space. She thumbed through the play money and the colored poker chips, and then plopped down on a leather sofa chair, contemplating what life was like those many years ago.

The tune *America the Beautiful* overcame her, and soon the tune turned into song.

Just then, Manu appeared, tucked in the right-hand corner,

legs crossed in a standing position, both surprising and embarrassing her, and thwarting her solo performance.

"Oh, please keep singing," he said, instructing her. "You have such a pretty voice. I usually don't like visiting this building, but your singing drew me in."

"Thanks," she responded timidly. This time she didn't feel like running away, but she didn't know how to talk to him either. So she ignored him for a bit, until he pleaded enough times to make her sing, convincing her to start from the beginning. She was happy to take his lead because it was easier than initiating a conversation.

When she got to the "America, America" part, she felt another presence behind her, at which point she whipped around, only to find Kenai standing there. Again, she stopped singing.

"Oh, don't stop," he said, and walked in front of her.

"Rose," Kenai repeated, trying to penetrate her paralysis. "Rose."

"Give her a minute," Manu said.

Kenai turned around, and saw Manu.

"I'm sorry...I didn't see you standing there," Kenai apologized. "I was too excited to find Rose singing here."

"You can see and hear him, too?" Rose blurted out.

"Why couldn't I?" Kenai asked, acting cool.

"Yeah," Manu teased, "Why couldn't he?"

"Wait, wait..." she started. "You know he's a....he's a....?" She felt a bit misplaced, then defensive, as if she were the last one in on the joke.

"A spirit?" Kenai completed her question.

"Yeah," she answered, more calmed now, impressed by his gentle use of 'spirit.' She had been referring to him as a ghost in her mind, and 'spirit' seemed much kinder, easier, more realistic to her somehow.

"I've been able to communicate with spirits since I can remember," he said.

"And it doesn't scare you?"

"Not really," he said.

"Does anyone know about it?"

"Not really. I mean, I did tell my parents, and they seemed cool with it, but I'm not sure they really believe me, you know. But they wouldn't ever say that. They're real nice, you know, and they asked me a few questions about it…"

"Like what?"

"Like, did I see them often? Was I friends with them? Did they scare me?"

"And, what did you tell them?"

"I told them that I see them once in awhile, and they're usually really nice, and don't bother me."

"And that was it?" Rose asked, flabbergasted.

"Yeah," Kenai said. "That was enough for them to know for some reason."

"And they didn't call you crazy?" she asked in astonishment.

"Why would they call me crazy?" he asked, confused.

"Forget it….How old were you when you first saw one?"

"Can't remember. Seems like I've always been able to see them. It's just something I do, you know, and it doesn't make me feel any different than I already do."

"You feel different?" she asked without thinking. Of course, she knew what he meant, but like everyone else, kind of tried to ignore his racial difference in their mostly Anglo and Latino population.

"C'mon," he said, in a reassuringly intimate way.

"Okay," she said with her head lowered. "I'm sorry, I didn't mean to say it like that."

"It's fine," he said. "I just kind of thought you were different in some way, too."

"I am!" she exclaimed, alarmed that she had become animated so suddenly, as if she had been waiting her entire life to admit to someone that she was, in fact, different without being judged for it, expecting someone, somewhere, somehow to recognize her strangeness as something good, not something she needed to hide, or pretend away.

"You two are a funny pair," Manu interrupted, startling them both. They had forgotten for a moment that he was still there with them.

"Sorry…" Rose began, walking towards Manu.

"Don't worry. People dismiss me all the time. I'm used to it," Manu replied.

"Have you met Manu before?" Rose asked Kenai. "I mean, Manuele. Manu's his nickname."

"I've seen you around," Kenai said directly to Manu. "But we've never talked. You're a shy one, aren't you?" he confirmed with the spirit.

"No, I just prefer pretty girls with beautiful voices," Manu said.

"Hey, watch it," Kenai warned, and they all giggled.

"What's your story?" Kenai asked Manu.

"My story?" Manu asked, taken aback by Kenai's confidence.

"Yeah, your story. You all seem to have one, but I can never get too much out of any of you."

"Is that so?" Manu asked, moving away from the corner and sitting on the pool table.

"Yeah," Kenai continued. "I've read a lot about what happened here, but I keep feeling I don't have the whole story. Like there's a big part missing, and I don't know what it is, and no one will even get close to telling me about it."

"A lot did happen here, and then it didn't," Manu responded. "And that's about the whole story."

"Yeah, right," Kenai sneered. "Let's go, Rose," Kenai said, obviously playing a game with Manu, trying to pull more information from him. Rose winked at Kenai, making him smile.

Booming voices and heavy footsteps projected from the stairwell.

Kenai pulled Rose towards the steps just as a couple of large men came barreling downstairs. The children let the men pass them then turned around, quietly following the men down again to check on Manu's status. But of course Manu had already departed.

Rose and Kenai realized that they were holding hands, and they let go simultaneously. They each wiped their warm hand on their own pants.

Rose hurried up the steps with Kenai close behind. He followed her all the way to the top landing, past the antique shoe-shining lounge chair, down the hallway pinned with quail drawings, to a tiny secret window that peered down on the Inn's front entrance with its ordered flags, knight-in-shining-armor-with-bird-on-his-lap sculpture made of old car bumpers set in the middle of the cul-de-sac, with a backdrop of the rolling river and emptied town in their view.

They pushed their noses against the paned glass, and gazed at the protective red rocks that had influenced Redstone's description as the "Ruby of the Rockies." They dared not hold hands again, but all of their fingers burned to reach out for one another. The magnetism between them peaked, pushing them apart with a jump. They made small talk as they found their way to the main floor, in front of the looming portrait of Alma Regina Shelgrem Osgood hanging on the landing between the first and main floors.

"I'm sure my parents are wondering where I am," Rose lied as they stood before the rack of postcards at the bottom of the stairs by the bar room.

"You sure you don't want to come in?" Kenai motioned to where his parents and sister were waiting for their dinner.

"No, that's okay, thanks," she said.

"They don't bite," he assured her. "They're really nice."

"I know," she said. "I just have to go." And she turned and headed for the double French doors.

"See ya soon," he raised his voice so she would be sure to hear him.

"Of course," she responded, checking out the receptionist at the front who knew her dad well. She just about skipped as she left the building, until she reached the design shop at the head of Redstone's main entrance, where her mom always bought holiday gifts for her family.

Rose had forgotten her bike, and ran back up to the front circle at the Redstone Inn to collect it. There was lingering daylight. She could still make the Fourth of July fireworks in Carbondale, the main town about twenty miles down the highway, that is, if her parents would agree to take her.

"That highway's just too dangerous to be driving up and down on the Fourth," her parents reminded her.

"I know, I know, but I really want to see the fireworks this year," she whined.

"Then you should have made arrangements to spend the night in town," her mom said matter-of-factly.

"I know," Rose exhaled, her body deflating under her.

"What, Rosie? Why such an attitude again?" her mother scolded.

"I'm sorry," Rose conceded, as usual.

"Let's go for a walk, Rosie," her dad said. "Maybe we can hear the band playing."

Her mom made a long face.

Why don't you join us, Susie?" her dad asked.

"That's okay," Susie said, folding her arms across her chest, acting more the child than Rose.

"No, let's go," her dad insisted. "Now."

So Susie, Joe and Rose strolled down Redstone Boulevard together, all the time Rose shuffling her feet.

They made it to the café, and chit-chatted in the driveway with a group of patrons. A bunch of them were tossing beanbags into animal-painted target holes and taking the game very seriously. Rose caught her mom lost in thought many times, staring at her waterproof sandals, kicking the pebbles around her feet. It had been about ten minutes when Susie signaled Joe that it was time to go. He was ready to leave as well, and they strolled back towards their house, waving goodnight to the pastor who was sitting on his front stoop with his matching wife, both of them in pattern-coordinated flannel shirts.

"Can we walk to the firehouse?" Rose asked.

"Oh, I don't know, RoRo," her mom began. "It's getting late now."

"Your mom's right, Ro," her dad agreed. "Let's go home and watch a movie," which is exactly what they did.

"You'll really like this one, Rosie," her mom said sweetly. "It's about aliens, came out when I was a kid. It's one of my all-time-favorites." Rose scrunched her nose at her mom.

"Or how about this one, about a man in love with his dead wife's ghost? You pick. They're both on cable tonight." Susie enjoyed sharing music and movies from her youth with Rose; it was one of the few ways she knew how to connect with her daughter.

"How about this one?" Rose suggested, pointing to a title in the movie guide magazine next to a picture of a funny-looking guy sitting on a park bench.

"That's strange, I just happened to watch that one the other night," Susie replied. "I don't think I can watch it again so soon. Life is definitely not like a box of chocolates to me," she said, referencing the movie. "So, which one will it be, the alien or the ghost movie?"

Neither Rose nor Joe offered their opinions, since in the end they both knew it wouldn't make a difference.

"Fine, the alien movie it is," her mom announced.

Rose was relieved. Watching the movie about a ghost would've been much too weird for her and unsettling tonight, especially sitting between her disjointed parents.

By the end of the movie, both of her parents had retreated to their room, and were now fast asleep. She went to the front porch, staring up at the endless sea of dots in the midnight sky, with the Big and Small Dipper beckoning her, as if to say, "You know, everything's going to be alright."

She began humming a wishful song from a movie about a puppet boy who's transformed into a real child as images of Kenai drifted across her mind.

The street had been quiet for at least twenty minutes when she spotted Kenai walking right past her house.

"Hey, Kee!" she whisper-yelled.

"Hi, Rose," he replied in a solemn voice.

"What's up?" she asked, letting go of her infatuated feelings and replacing them with a kind of motherly love for him.

"Nothing," he lied.

"C'mon," she pushed.

"I don't know," he began. "I'm upset, I guess, but I don't really know why. I mean, I do know why, but I feel like I don't really have the right to be upset, if that makes any sense."

"It does. But why don't you feel like you have a right to be upset? Everyone has a right to be upset once in awhile. Ask my mom, she thinks she has the right to be upset all the time," Rose laughed to herself.

"The thing is, I just don't know where these feelings come from. It's like I'm alright for awhile, and then all of a sudden, I get upset, really upset."

"Wanna sit down?" Rose asked him, patting the space on the porch stairs next to her.

"Sure," Kenai answered, pulling his shoulders up.

"What made you upset today?" she asked him. "It's okay if you don't want to tell me, though."

"No, that's okay. Just something my grandma said, about my dad's brother. Made me think of my birth parents, I guess," Kenai said.

"So you remember them, your birth parents?" Rose asked.

"No, I don't think so," Kenai said. "I just kind of imagine them sometimes. I lived at an orphanage in Kenya for almost a year before my parents adopted me. They visited me many times, they say, but weren't able to bring me to America for a little while. I don't remember any of this, though, but they tell me that I'm not very affectionate because I wasn't held as much as I should've been during my first year."

"That's sad," Rose said.

"But my birth parents aren't dead, you know, just very, very poor," Kenai responded in defense of himself. "I might meet them one day, when I'm older, if I want to, if they want to."

"So, will you want to meet them, your birth parents?"

"Yeah, I think so," Kenai said. "But I don't want to make too much of a big deal about it now, you know, because it kind of hurts my mom and dad for them to think about, even if they don't admit it. I used to thank them for being my parents, for saving me and giving me such a good life, but they didn't like that, either. They think we're all meant to be together. They say there's no reason to thank them, it was all in God's hands from the beginning, and for some reason we can't know, or aren't supposed to know why God put us half way across the world to find each other."

"That's so sweet," Rose said, looking deeply into Kenai's eyes by then. It was dark outside even with the shining stars, and the gentle night breeze enveloped them.

"I know, it is nice," Kenai responded. "But you see then why I feel so bad about being sad sometimes?" Kenai stood up abruptly. "I gotta go," he said. "I really shouldn't be out here so late. But I'm happy you were here. Really. Thanks, Rose." He put his hands in his sweatshirt pocket and began swinging his elbows.

"No worries," she said, kicking her feet around. She sat up straight, about to stand, but then slumped back down again.

"Sweet dreams, Rose," Kenai said, taking a few steps towards his house.

"You, too, Kee. Don't let the bed bugs bite," she said, moving her body in Kenai's direction.

"If you do, hit 'em with a shoe, until they're black and blue," he replied, pounding his fist up and down in the air.

They both laughed.

Kenai took a few more steps towards home when he turned back suddenly. Rose was standing on her porch by then, ready to go back inside.

"Rose!" he whisper-yelled her way.

"What?"

"Nothing," he said with a twisted grin.

"It's okay," she said. "Goodnight. I'll see you later."

"Yeah. Goodnight," Kenai said, and skip-walked back home, without looking back this time. She did the same, skip-walking into her house without looking back towards the street again that night.

They both stayed awake in their own beds for about an hour, replaying their conversation over and over in their minds, until pure exhaustion eventually wore them out.

 few days later Rose came upon Kenai at the ice cream shop. His bike was parked outside, and so she took the liberty to park her bike alongside his and say hello. He was ordering a mint chocolate chip ice cream cone.

"Hi Rose!" Kenai exclaimed. "What flavor do you want?"

"I swear, I wanted mint chocolate chip, not just 'cause you do," she said quickly, and then blushed.

They each ordered mint chocolate chip ice cream and then meandered onto the shop's stone patio overlooking the river. The water was low this year; the white and grey rocks were jutting out of the ground, dry halfway out like stepping stones.

"I really want to know more about Manu, don't you?" Rose asked.

"I know. Me, too," Kenai agreed.

"Do you think he's easy to find? I mean, I always just run into him," Rose said. "I never ask for him, you know what I mean?"

"I know exactly what you mean," Kenai said, and turned his head to the side. Rose became a bit shy, too, but not enough so that it stopped the conversation.

"How do you think we could find him?"

"I don't know. Maybe we should go back to one of the places we've seen him, and just ask for him?"

"Just like that?"

"Well, why not?"

"How many times have you seen him before?" Rose asked Kenai.

"A couple times a year, I guess. I only see him when he's walking the streets, in a pretty gloomy mood. I wouldn't say that would be the best place to call for him. He seemed much happier around you, at the Inn."

"I've also seen him down by the beach, by the big boulder, you know where I'm talking about?" Rose asked.

"Of course."

"So, which place should we go?"

"I don't know, how about the boulder?" Kenai suggested.

"Let's go," Rose said.

"But we have our cones, hard to bike with them. Let's just walk to the Inn."

Kenai and Rose stood up at the same time, and headed back through the shop, towards the front. He opened the door for her, and she grinned back at him.

"Thanks," she said. "You don't have to do that you know, open the door for me."

"I know," he replied. "But I like doing it."

She didn't know how to respond to his kindness, so she just picked up her bike with her free hand and moved it next to Kenai's. "We can just come back and get them later," she said.

They began walking towards the Inn together. She dropped her hand near his, but then pulled her arm up when she saw one of her dad's fishing buddies heading towards them.

Rose and Kenai were silent for most of the walk, enjoying the cool breezes and watching the motorcycles and RVs roll down the boulevard.

As they neared the Inn with their ice cream cones finished, save for a few drops around their mouths and T-shirts, they scurried inside like field mice, past the elk and deer and moose heads on the walls of the fireplace room, and down the stairs to the game room. They stood beside the pool table, and looked at one another.

"Now what?" Kenai asked.

"Maybe we just ask for him….Manu? Manu?" she called, turning around in circles, hoping that the projection of her voice would reach whichever dimension necessary to get his attention. But there was no response.

"Manuele? Man-uel-ay!" Kenai said louder.

"Manu, would you please come out and talk to us? We want to learn more about you. Please," Rose asked as delicately as she possibly could.

But still nothing.

"Oh, this is silly," Kenai gave up, and turned toward the stairs.

"No, let's think," Rose pleaded. "I know we can figure this out together."

"Well, how did he come the other times?"

"The first time I was just sitting on the rock, minding my own business, singing softly to myself, and then…"

"That's it, of course!" Kenai said. "You have to sing!"

"Sing?"

"Yes, sing. I remember the last time we were in here you were singing when I found you."

"I was?"

"Yeah, you don't remember? *America the Beautiful?* He liked your voice, don't you remember? I loved it, too."

"You really think that's it?" she asked shyly.

"Just try," he encouraged her.

Rose moved to the middle of the room, and closed her eyes. She rubbed her hands together, took a deep breath, and began her song. *O beautiful for spacious skies,* she projected, imagining herself atop one of those mighty mountains, overlooking the free rivers, the green outlines of the aspens, the dance of the deer, the expanse of it all, *for amber waves of grain, for purple mountains majesty, above the fruited plains, America, America, God shed Her grace on thee, and crown thy good with sisterhood, from sea to shining sea!*

"Sisterhood?" a deep voice asked. It was Manu, slouched in the corner.

Rose opened her eyes, her hands sweaty, "Um, um, yeah, I guess, I changed the word so long ago, I kind of forgot about it," she explained, her voice shaking. "It didn't make much sense to me," she continued, "singing about 'brotherhood,' when I'm a girl, and the person who wrote the poem was a woman, and any-way, it's the boys who usually fight, like in wars, I just think, well, 'sisterhood' goes better with the song."

"That's a very mature thought for such a young person," Manu said.

Staring at the walls, Rose responded, "I guess so…I get that a lot."

There was silence, and then Rose elaborated, "It's just the way I am. I know I'm too serious, that I think too much. I always have. But it's just the way I am, I can't help it."

"I think it's awesome," Kenai piped in.

"You do?" Rose blurted out, turning around to see Kenai sitting in one of the antique wood chairs. "Really?" she asked again.

"I do," he said.

"Me, too," Manu agreed.

Rose blushed, her chest warm with red blotches. She almost felt like crying. No one had ever been so considerate of her before.

"So, Manu, we wanted to know more about you," Rose said. "Is that okay? Can we ask you some questions?"

"Only if you want to, really, we don't mean to intrude," Kenai added.

"It's fine," Manu acquiesced. "I think it's time anyway. I'm getting real tired of hanging around this place. All I do is go over and over in my mind what happened here, and I can't seem to shake it."

Manu moved to the card table and sat down while Rose and Kenai kept their places. They glanced at each other with wide eyes, holding their breath.

After a minute or so of watching Manu brood with his head resting on his fist, eyes drooping a bit, Rose asked, "How did you get to Redstone? I mean, were you born here?"

"No, I wasn't. I was almost twelve, about your age, when we moved here."

"From where?"

"Trinidad...Trinidad, Colorado. We lived there for about three years before moving to Redstone."

"And before that?" Rose asked, which opened the door for Manu to tell his story.

He said his family hailed from a small town in Southern Italy, a place he hardly remembered. A couple of his uncles had already come to America, and his parents wanted to join them. They heard there was a lot of work and money in America, and they wanted to be a part of it. So, Manu, his mother and father, older brother and baby sister got on a boat for America, arriving at Ellis Island in New York City, and then a few months later took a train to Colorado.

"I think they considered staying in New York because it was such an exciting place to be," Manu added, "but with my papa's brothers in Colorado, they headed west soon enough."

His uncles were shoemakers in Trinidad, and they had their own store. His father went to work for his uncles for awhile, but with three children and then another one on the way, he wanted to make more money than his older brothers could pay him. He learned about working the mines, and as he was a large and formidable man, he first took a job at Cokedale, just outside of Trinidad, but then took a job with the Colorado Fuel and Iron Company's new camp at Primero, a little farther outside of Trinidad. He soon learned to pull ovens, making more money for the family who remained living in Trinidad.

"He did really well, everyone liked my papa, and my papa, being a big talker who spoke English pretty well, too, heard about Redstone; they called it 'The Ruby of the Rockies,' and it was the best place to be, especially for a family. Soon enough, my papa was transferred here, and we got to live in a house on the boulevard, because he became one of the managers," Manu said.

"Which house? Is it still standing?" Rose asked while shivers ran down her leg.

Manu was quiet for a moment. "Yes," he said, looking at Rose. "Your house. That was my house. And your room, that's where me and my brother and sisters slept."

"I thought you said that was the Wright house! Why did you lie to me? Why have I never seen you there before?" Rose accosted Manu, raising her voice while pulling her hands up to her chest and shuffling her feet back a few steps.

"I didn't lie. The Wrights lived there before us, until they needed a bigger house. But I never wanted you to see me there. I thought it would scare you too much, and I see it has."

And with that, Manu disappeared.

Kenai stamped his foot and crossed his arms. Tears gathered at the corner of Rose's eyes. She ran towards the stairs, and climbed them as fast as her feet would take her. She shot out of the Inn, and raced back to her bike, which was waiting for her at the ice cream shop.

Kenai tried to chase after Rose, but when he realized she was running too fast to want to wait for him, he slowed down to a trot. He turned around and headed back into the Inn, directly for the library, paying no attention to the people milling around in the foyer. He studied the seven paintings on the wall, all by Frank Mechau. Kenai especially loved the 1936 painting of Glenwood Springs' Red Mountain. The deep reds and aging lines from the face of the mountain contrasted with the soft blues of the sky and shadows reminded Kenai of a time before now, when meadows and farmlands filled the rural landscape instead of a strip mall and other commercial buildings.

The other paintings, colored mostly with muted blues, greys, yellows and reds and featuring wild and tamed horses, took Kenai's mind away from Rose, and towards his own vague memories of the local past, as if he had somehow been a part of it then. He tried to conjure up some past life, but nothing came to him besides a general feeling of familiarity and comfort.

He stayed in the library for twenty or thirty minutes, gazing out the window, watching the cars drive up to the entrance circle, the guests sauntering in, the cars driving away, the guests sauntering away, until it seemed enough time had passed, and he was ready to go home, alone. The woman at the front desk, his neighbor's grandmother, smiled and waved goodbye to him on his way out.

When Rose eventually got home, she saw Mechau curled up on the porch. She kneeled for Mechau to come towards her, and the little fox walked right into her arms. Rose cuddled him and let her tears flow, stroking Mechau slowly, petting his soft paws and rubbing his sleek yet soft ears between her fingers.

"I didn't mean to scare him, I didn't mean to scare him," she sobbed. "What an idiot I am, such a stupid idiot, a stupid, stupid idiot." She continued to berate herself, petting Mechau until her sobs turned into normal breathing.

The light from the sun encircled the giant cloud resting above them, until the cloud moved away to make room for rays that streamed down onto the little girl and her beloved fox. It warmed her face and dried the wetness. She soothed herself into daydreaming, until the opening of the creaky front screened door, and Mechau's sudden jumping off from her lap, startled her.

Her mom was coming outside for a smoke. Rose wiped her

eyes, and brushed past her mom, mumbling. "I'm hungry," she said.

"Well, you're old enough to fix yourself something, you know."

"I know," Rose replied, and slipped into her house. She grabbed the last green apple from the fruit bowl and went into her room, once Manu and his siblings' room, and envisaged how they had fit four kids into that limited space. It wasn't like they had many books or toys back then, she thought. Suddenly a twinge of gratitude for all the things she had ran through her body until it became a moment of happiness.

From the upper shelf, she pulled her drawing pad and pastels that her favorite aunt had sent for her last birthday. The colors were vibrant and unique, not an array of the typical hues she had to use at school. She started slowly, letting the pastels show her what she needed to express. She experimented with different shapes and color combinations, and tried to cover every inch of the page with her imagination. No distinct images came to her, but rather patterns and disruptions from the patterns.

Being a lefty, she worked hard not to smudge the paper with the pinky-side of her left hand. She drew for an hour, then tore her creation from the sketchpad, tacking it onto her oversized corkboard, next to all her other drawings. She rested on her bed, her hands behind her head, staring in wonder at her artwork. The images she had finished many years ago no longer felt like they had come from her.

*T*he afternoon thunderstorms cooled down the days, a sure sign that summer was ending. A dampness filled the open spaces, while hints of yellow appeared on the periphery of scattered aspen leaves.

Today Rose walked directly to Kenai's front gate, onto the paved stones, up the three steps to the deck, and knocked on the door. It was mid-morning during the second week of August, about a week after she had last seen Kenai, and she didn't care who saw her there.

She admired the pretty landscaping around Kenai's house, the varied flowers and bushes, and wished she knew all their scientific and common names. She should know their names, she thought to herself, but no one had taught her, no less showed her, how to garden. She recognized the Indian Paintbrushes, however. Their orange-red tips and yellow insides were easy to spot, and they carried their own myth about an Indian brave who tried to paint the sunset with his war paints: the Indian brave had asked the Great Spirit for help because he couldn't make his painting as beautiful as Nature, so the Great Spirit gave him paintbrushes of all colors of the rainbow. The grateful brave painted his masterpieces with his new brushes, and then discarded them in the fields, from which these beautiful flowers grew.

Kenai's mom answered the door. She had auburn hair, ocean green eyes, and olive skin, with a toothy smile that seemed to reach both earlobes. His toddler sister Desta, with pink ribbons wrapped around pigtails shooting out from both sides of her head, was holding onto her mom's leg.

"Hi," Rose said. "I'm Rose, and um, I was wondering, is Kenai home?"

"Hi, Rose," she replied. "I'm Naomi. I've heard a lot about you."

"You have?"

"Of course," she said. "Come in."

"I love your garden," Rose said as she entered the house, stepping lightly on the teakwood floor.

"Thank you," Naomi said. "Kenai!" she called up the stairs. "Your friend is here to see you." As Naomi tried to move out of the doorway, Desta held on tighter.

Kenai ran down the stairs and smiled when he saw Rose.

"Hi," he welcomed her. "Let's go," he said, and took her hand to lead her out the door.

"Don't you want to show her around the house?" his mom suggested, stopping them in their tracks.

"Maybe later, Mom. Is it okay if we go out for a little bit first?"

"Of course, but you know, be back by six, okay? For supper. It's Friday night," she reminded him.

"What're we having?" Kenai asked.

"Veggie and tofu lasagna. Rose, would you like to join us for supper?"

"Oh, that's nice," Rose replied off-guard. "I don't know. I'd have to ask my parents."

"Well, just join us if you can, we have plenty. See you later." Naomi waved goodbye to her son and his new friend, but they were down the porch steps too fast to notice.

"Your mom is really so nice," Rose said to Kenai who returned her comment with a sidewise grin. They began walking towards the Inn, both knowing exactly where they wanted to go without a single mention of it.

"I know. Hey, I'm sorry about last week. I didn't mean to get mad."

"I know; I was just really embarrassed about scaring Manu. I felt really bad about it."

"Don't," he reassured her. "It's not like dealing with spirits comes with a manual. Or a Manuele."

They both laughed at Kenai's pun, and at the same time noticed a golden-mantled squirrel mangled on the side of the road.

"I hate seeing that," Rose said under her breath.

"Me, too," Kenai agreed, turning his head away from the carcass.

Rose realized soon after that they were holding hands. She let go abruptly. Just then a great blue heron darted across the sky, swooping down towards the river.

The sky was overcast with dark grey rain clouds hovering in the distance. The children picked up their pace. The Inn's manager was strolling her newborn down the road and greeted them both. Rose and Kenai veered right where the road curved towards the highway, then crossed to the gravel parking lot, up along the side porch, and in the poolside door, skirting around the restaurant kitchen and the fireplace room, down the stairs to the game room.

"Why don't you sing this time?" Rose asked Kenai.

"Oh, no, he only likes your voice."

"How do you know that?"

"I tried once and it didn't work," he explained.

"Okay," she said. "But do you think I can pick another song?"

"Like what?"

"I don't know. How about *Amazing Grace*? Do you know that one?"

"Of course. Who doesn't know *Amazing Grace*?"

Rose was able to get through the entire song before Manu appeared. She pretended she was on a church pulpit in the middle of a large prairie with people swaying back and forth like wheat. He was thoroughly enjoying the song and didn't want to interrupt her. But when he finally allowed his spirit to materialize, he was wearing a different outfit. It was formal wear of some sort, but the children didn't want to question him too much about it, trying to play their cards just right so he'd stay for a long time today. It was still early morning and they both had nowhere to go or be until dinnertime.

"Hi, Manu," Rose began. "I'm sorry, we're both sorry, about last time."

"It's okay," he admitted. "I'm just not used to this whole communication thing, with you living people."

Kenai and Rose both nodded their heads, and asked Manu to continue his story.

"Here, sit," Manu said, pointing to a couple of chairs around the card table. He sat down in another one, and continued his story where he had last left it. They felt their time all together was limited and precious, and wanted to take advantage of every moment.

He told them that he was eleven when his family arrived in Redstone. His father didn't want him to work in the mines with him, he wanted better for his sons, but Manu wanted to work and didn't like reading books so much, so he found a job working in the castle. He started as a dishwasher in the kitchen. His father helped get him the job, even though he really wanted him to study. That's when Manuele first saw her, the first time he had ever seen her face-to-face, and once he did, he knew he wanted to be around her all the time.

"I think we were all in love with her. It was strange, because I was so young, I know, and I didn't know I could feel that way being a kid, but I did. How could you not be? Not only was she radiantly beautiful with her soft honey blond hair and her bright blue eyes, but her whole face was so kind, so gentle, *bellisima, bellisima,* and she had this delicate yet powerful voice, I didn't know women could be like that, especially in America," Manu said.

"*In Italia,* everyone is crazy about love, *pazzi per amore,* while in America everyone is crazy about money and power. I learned that very quickly, no one ever talked about love here, they talked about this job, that job, having this, having that, it's what brought us all to America, I know, but in *Italia,* it was *sem-*

pre about love, romance, *amore*, which I only started to appreciate once we moved here."

Manu fell into a kind of trance, recalling his childhood in Redstone with unbounded energy. He spoke of his parents, who liked to kiss a lot until they started to feel strange about it once they lived in America, and over time, they almost became American, not kissing in public, even though his father could never completely stop hugging his mother in front of other people. Manu recalled how embarrassing it was for him, but it also made him proud, too, to know how much they loved each other.

"So when I saw her, I wanted to hug her like that, touch the golden light all around her, but I didn't, *naturalmente*, I didn't. All I wanted to do was be around her, *sempre*, always, around her," he said.

Manu became further lost in his recollections, and the children felt the need to bring him back to them after several moments had passed them by.

"Who was she, the woman you're talking about?" they asked in unison.

"Oh, yes," he returned. "Mrs. Osgood. Alma Regina. Soul Queen. Queen of my Soul. Alma Regina Shelgrem Osgood. We called her 'Lady Bountiful.' And she was."

Manu explained to the children that Lady Bountiful was the second wife of John Cleveland Osgood, the man responsible for Redstone. She was as gentle as he was harsh. She cared very much for all the people, and she would bring the villagers gifts from Chicago and New York for the holidays. She listened to everybody and worked very hard to keep everything afloat.

When she and Mr. Osgood finally had to leave Redstone for good, Manu said that he begged to go with her. He wanted to see the world and leave the small town life of Redstone behind him. But she wouldn't take anyone with her; she couldn't. She was broken-hearted and needed to find her way again. Manu couldn't stand her being gone. He, like most everyone during that time, believed that Redstone would never be the same without her.

"The town kind of died the day she left," Manu said in a weepy voice. "And I think to this day has never fully recovered."

He sounded as if he were about to cry, and perhaps he was crying, but spirits couldn't really make tears so it was hard to tell one way or the other.

The children weren't sure what to say or do next. They wanted to learn a lot more; this was surely only the beginning. But they had learned to stay quiet when there was a heavy mood, and so all of them sat for a few minutes together in complete silence.

Manu eventually raised his head and looked directly at the children. "Do you want to hear more?" he asked.

"Oh, yes!" Rose exclaimed, quickly covering her mouth with her hand to apologize for the outburst.

Kenai finished for her, "We could sit here for hours if you'd let us."

"Then let us go somewhere more private. I am afraid people will come down here any minute and bother us. *Va bene?* Is that okay?" Manu suggested.

"Absolutely," Kenai agreed. "Where should we go?"

"I like that spot by the river, where Rose....where we first met. Do you remember?" he asked her directly.

"That's my favorite place to go. I hardly see anyone there, ever," Rose said.

Manu disappeared while the children made their way to the other side of town. On the way, they saw what they assumed to be the same blue heron they had spotted just a little while ago. Now the heron, with its sturdy, yellow legs, stood erect in the river, pretending to be the tall grass in order to catch a fish. In a flash, the bird catapulted its head into the water, and burst up with the prey in its long beak. The heron paused for a few moments, waiting until the fish stopped wiggling in its mouth, and then tossed it into the air, catching the trout headfirst, swallowing it whole.

Thunder crackled in the distance without a sign of lightning. Rose and Kenai ran to get their bikes at home. It wasn't going to rain, they prayed. Often the sky threatened to storm, but wouldn't follow through with its warning. Kenai would have to sneak his bike, because his mother definitely would not allow him to ride around with the possibility of lightning. He escaped well enough, and the two of them raced each other down the back road, past the fire station, just beyond the double campsites, the one farther down the road named for Mr. Osgood himself. By the time they had reached their magic spot, the sky had cleared into a robin's egg blue, with only jet streams of clouds remaining.

*N*estled against a couple of blue spruces jutting out from the
red rock, Rose and Kenai looked around for their friend.
They wanted to see if he would come as he had promised, without
the call of a song. Indeed, he did, and this time, he sat beside them,
now dressed in summer casual clothes, his white shirt rolled up to
his elbows, and his khaki trousers pulled up to his knees.

"Do you know the story of Redstone, and about the coal
mines all over Colorado?" he asked the children.

"A little bit," Kenai replied.

"Yeah, a little bit," Rose seconded.

"What do you know?"

"I know that Mr. Osgood owned a company that made fuel
from the coal in the ground."

"And where did they get the coal? What did they use it for?" Manu asked pedantically, a style of speech he had inherited from Lady Bountiful.

"The miners would pull the coal from the mines up by Coal Basin Road, and then shovel it in the coke ovens to make it easier to use and travel with. They'd load the coke onto the trains, and sell the coal around the country. People burned the coke to make energy for heat, mostly."

"And what's the coal actually made from? How come there's so much energy in it?"

"Fossils, I think," Rose said. "Millions of years of plants and animals turning into fossils. There's a lot of energy stored up in dead things, I guess," she deducted.

"*Touché*," Manu joked.

"What does that mean?" Rose asked.

"Oh nothing, I'm sorry. I was making fun of myself, really. You were talking about energy and dead things," Manu clarified.

"Oh," Rose replied, not sure if she should laugh or apologize.

"Don't worry, you're a very smart girl," Manu complimented her. Rose blushed.

"Well, mining was very difficult and dangerous work." Manu continued teaching the children. He talked to them about how a lot of people died in the mines, and how the miners weren't treated well. They came from all over the world, from Italy, England, Ireland, France, Belgium, Germany, Bulgaria, Greece, Poland, Croatia, Mexico, even Japan, Korea, and China to work here. Like his parents, they had heard that there were plenty of jobs available mining coal and making coke, and lots of money to be made. Almost everyone believed in the American Dream then. What they didn't know before arriving at their new destination, though, was how little the companies paid them, how bad their living conditions were, how dangerous the work was.

"The company men wanted all the money for themselves, and the way to make the most money was to pay the workers as little as possible," Manu said.

"I think it's still that way today," Rose added astutely.

"Really? That's a shame," Manu rejoined. "Well, in my day, many of the workers tried to get together to form a union. Do you know what a union is?"

"I do," Kenai said, instinctually raising his hand.

"You don't have to raise your hand, Kenai. This is not a classroom," Manu said, making them all giggle. "But tell me, what is a union?"

"A union is when workers get together to fight for their rights. They think if a lot of them get together, the companies will listen to them better than if they just speak up as individuals," Kenai explained.

"Exactly," Manu said. "And sometimes the unions got so big, the government would get involved."

Manu explained that the men running the big companies, and especially Osgood, did not like unions, and wanted to ensure that none of them formed at all. These businessmen wouldn't allow people who spoke the same language to live too close together in order to prevent self-organizing. The more people could talk to one another about how badly they were being treated and paid, the more powerful they theoretically could become.

Osgood fought almost harder than anyone to prevent the unions from forming, and to break them apart. Some say he was doing it on the workers' behalf, but most people just thought he was a real bully. Ironically, that was Redstone's main inspiration and purpose, to show how well Osgood treated his workers, and that if he created a beautiful town where workers could live a good life, they wouldn't want to unionize, because they wouldn't feel any need to. Osgood believed that the men should be able to work as many hours as they wanted, and to earn as much money as they wanted, without any union rules. Redstone became a social experiment, then, and Osgood even brought in a doctor, not a medical doctor but someone who studies people and societies, a sociologist, to help make Redstone a very special place. Lady Bountiful, of course, was one of the leaders in the experiment; she wanted it to work more than anyone. But she had a different intention than her greedy husband. She wanted to do good.

"Was Mr. Osgood mean to her, too?" Rose asked.

"Not really," Manu responded thoughtfully. "Well, yes, he could be really mean to her, that's what she told me in secret, but she also said he loved her a lot. He was always very nice to her in public, so I never saw him be too mean. He would just bark at her sometimes, you know, but then he would catch himself, and be all *gentile* again. He knew he couldn't let people see him being rude to her, because she was the one who kept the whole town together."

"You really think he loved her, though?" Rose asked.

"I do," Manu admitted. "In his own way, he did. But he didn't have much love in his heart, you know. He lost his parents when he was young, and I think that made him a very hard and lonely person. She definitely loved him in the beginning, *voglio dire*, I don't think she never stopped loving him, but I think she just couldn't take his cruelty anymore. She came here with a dream, and when that dream fell apart, she did, too."

"How did you get to know her so well?" Kenai asked.

Manu reimagined his first encounter with Mrs. Osgood. As soon as he saw her, he did everything he could to take care of her and her guests. He always arrived early and left late, and never complained. He made sure his clothes and hair always looked perfect, and even worked on his days off if she needed him. She didn't oversee the kitchen staff, she had a manager for that, but he knew she was the kind of person who paid attention to every single detail, and so he acted as if she were always watching him.

"Yeah, because whenever she did see you, you were at your best, you were ready for her," Kenai said.

"Exactly, my boy. You, too, are a smart one. *Un ragazzo intelligente.* You will be very good with the ladies one day," Manu said. Both Kenai and Rose acknowledged this truth by turning their heads away from the other's gaze.

"About a year after I started working there, she got sick." Manu continued, describing how ill she was with typhoid fever. He volunteered to bring food and water into her room, salves for her itchy rashes, and cold compresses for her fever and headaches. As much as everyone loved her, they didn't want to get sick. Typhoid fever was contagious, but could be contained with adequate sanitation and hygiene, so Manu wasn't too worried. He believed the risk of infection was well worth spending time with Mrs. Osgood. The rest of the staff blamed her for her illness, saying she had spent too much time with the children of the mining camps.

It was not proper for a boy Manu's age to be helping her in this way, but he had insisted. During the first few days of her illness, he went in her room with one of the headmistresses of the house who asked Mrs. Osgood if it was suitable for him to be there. Mrs. Osgood said it would be fine in the afternoons, but not in the mornings or evenings. "I never understood why only in the afternoons, but suspected it had something to do with Mr. Osgood," Manu said.

As such, Manu tended to her in the afternoons, and by the fourth day, he was allowed to go in there alone. She was feeling a little better, especially with her stomach, but she still had fever and rashes, and was very tired. The doctor insisted she be on bed-rest for at least another two weeks, to ensure her full recovery. She wanted someone to read to her. She loved books, but felt too weak to read herself.

Manu then began to tell his story as if he had gone back in time, as if he were right there while narrating the scene playing out before him.

"'I'm sorry I look so horrid,'" Mrs. Osgood said. 'But for some reason, I don't feel ashamed around you. Why is that?'

"I blushed, and I could not provide her a proper answer. Then she asked me if I knew how to read English, in her very beautiful Swedish accent. They said that she was of Swedish royalty, a countess *forse*, which was not hard to believe.

"'Yes,' I replied, which was mostly the truth. I did know how to read, but just a little. At that moment, I wished I had listened to my father and studied my books. But then, I wouldn't have been standing in front of her at that moment if I had.

"'Fine, then,' she said. 'Will you read to me tomorrow? Anything from my shelf will be good.'

"'Do you mind if I choose now, so I can learn it well for you, *Signora?*' I asked.

"'That is a brilliant idea,' she said. 'Go and choose something then, Manuele. But don't tell me now. I want to be surprised tomorrow.'

"I stared at the shelf, and decided to follow wherever my eyes took me. I moved to the left, and looked to the middle shelf. I could hardly read the title at the time, but in order not to seem illiterate, I grabbed it from the shelf and placed it under my arm.

"'Careful,' she warned. 'I love my books more than almost anything. Please be gentle with them.'

"I felt like an idiot. How could I have been so rough with anything she had touched?

"'I am so sorry, *Signora*. Please forgive me,' I said. 'I feel honored that you have even let me touch any of your things.'

"'No need for dramatics,' she said kindly. 'I will see you tomorrow.'

"'Yes, ma'am,'" I bowed my head and left the room with the book safely tucked under my arm, pressed against my side, with my right hand holding it firmly in place. I left that room walking on air, convinced this had been the best moment of my life, the moment when she entrusted me with one of her books, with her love; tomorrow couldn't have come quickly enough. Now looking back at my short life, perhaps that *was* the best moment of my life, and I was only fourteen at the time.

"Arriving home, I begged my sister Adelina to teach me to read. She was the most intelligent of us, even though she was just eleven. She could see in my eyes how desperate I was. I had not always been the best brother to her, mostly ignoring her rather than teasing her, but she was a very good person, and wanted to be a schoolteacher when she grew up, so she worked with me until dinner, and then after our chores, until late in the evening. We were lucky to have electricity; Redstone was the first village of its kind to have so much, but I suppose that's why we were all working and living there in the first place."

"But which book did you chose?" Rose interrupted.

"Oh, yes, I was just getting to that. It was *Daniel Deronda* by George Eliot. Have you ever heard of this author?"

"No," Rose and Kenai answered. "We're only going into seventh grade."

"Well, George Eliot was actually a woman, and I hadn't heard of her either, but that wasn't saying much since I had never heard of anyone back then. George Eliot happened to be Mrs. Osgood's favorite. Lucky for me I had chosen to read such a good book, but unlucky for me that the reading was very difficult. I tried very hard that night with Adelina to read the first chapter, I even tried to memorize it, but I was still unsure of many of the words.

"When I arrived at work the next day, the headmistress informed me that Mrs. Osgood wanted to sleep all day, and didn't want any company. I wasn't sure how to take the news, but I tried not to get discouraged. During my breaks, I studied the book, and when I got home, Adelina helped me again.

"The next day, again Mrs. Osgood didn't want to see me, and this time I thought it was something I did or said. The headmistress said it wasn't about me, only that Mrs. Osgood wanted to be alone. I continued to study the book, and by the third day it came to me; the reading was much easier, and I could even go onto the next chapter with little help from Adelina. Papa had always told me I was a smart boy who could learn fast, but I never thought it would be true of books.

"The following day when Mrs. Osgood wanted to see me, finally, I almost ran up the stairs to her bedroom, hugging the book against my chest. I opened the door, very short of breath.

"'Manuele, are you alright?' Mrs. Osgood asked.

"'Oh, just fine,' I said catching my breath, 'but I should be asking you the same thing. Was it something I said or did that made you not want to see me?'

"'Of course not, my dear. I am seeing you now, aren't I? So, can we read together?'

"I pulled a chair up to her bed, and laid the book on my legs. I took a deep breath, and turned to the first page. '*The Spoiled Child*,' I said aloud. 'Oh!' she exclaimed. '*Daniel Deronda*! One of my very favorites! George Eliot was a genius, and a woman. Oh, that makes me think of Arthur. Poor, poor Arthur.'

"'Who is Arthur?' I asked her.

"'That is for another time. I'm sorry I interrupted you. Please continue,' she said.

"So I began to read, quite well I must say, for having just started to read. I could almost recite the first few paragraphs by heart.

"Can you recite them to us now?" Rose asked.

"I don't know. I suppose I could try. Let me see."

Manu searched for the words, and soon enough they began to flow:

"Men can do nothing without the make-believe of a beginning. Even science, the strict measurer, is obliged to start with a make-believe unit, and must fix on a point in the stars' unceasing journey when his sidereal clock shall pretend that time is at nought. His less accurate grandmother poetry has always been understood to start in the middle; but on reflection it appears that her proceeding is not

very different from his; since science, too, reckons backwards as well as forwards, divides his unit into billions, and with his clock-finger at nought really sets off 'in media res.' No retrospect will take us to the true beginning; and whether our prologue be in heaven or earth, it is but a fraction of that all-presupposing fact with which our story sets out."

"You remembered all of that?" Rose asked in disbelief.

"Well," Manu explained, "I guess it's not really remembering. I'm going back in time and reading alongside myself. It's kind of hard to explain, but I can actually see the words in front of me as I speak them."

"What do they all mean?" Kenai chimed in.

"I suppose it means different things to different people. You can never be quite sure what any author really means to say, but that doesn't matter either. It's how the words touch you that matters most. In my mind, I think Eliot was saying that science and words are more similar than we think, and that people somehow need a sense of time to make their lives real. But time is a creation, as is death. There is no beginning and no end."

"Wow," Rose said. "That's a lot to think about."

"It is, but it is worth considering, since most people spend their lives so afraid of death that they never live, but that may be too much for you young children to understand."

Rose and Kenai looked deeply into each other's eyes.

"But it is really the next paragraph that made my interaction with Mrs. Osgood that day so strange for me," Manu continued. "I tried to hide my feelings for her, but I think the redness on my face and neck gave me away."

"What did it say?" Rose asked.

Manu recited from memory again.

> **"Was she beautiful or not beautiful? And what was
> the secret form or expression, which gave the
> dynamic quality to her glance? Was the good or the
> evil genius dominant in those beams? Probably the
> evil; else why was the effect that of unrest rather
> than of undisturbed charm? Why was the wish to
> look again felt as coercion and not as a longing in
> which the whole being consents?**

"I continued reading until the end of the chapter, and read several more to her in the following days, but then she told me to finish the book myself, at home, which I did. When she became well, we discussed the chapters, the whole book actually, and then she gave me a long list of books to read, and it was through her that I became educated. I don't know why she picked me in particular to tutor, it was just the circumstances I guess, but it worked for both of us.

"Through the books, she told me a lot about herself, and her life at Cleveholm, which was their name for the castle. She didn't speak much about her life before coming to America, or even about when she was in New York or Denver; it was mostly about her life in Redstone. Often she revealed feelings that I don't think she meant to reveal, but I was her safest confidant, especially because I was so young and innocent. Mr. Osgood would never have approved of her spending so much time with anyone else, *per certo*, and our friendship kind of made up for his not being able to give her *bambini*."

A loud thunder clapped nearby followed by a few drops of rain falling on the children's hair and shoulders. Manu seemed to be fading in and out simultaneously, wavering between two worlds. Before they could say goodbye to him, he had faded out completely. They hopped on their bikes, and sped home, trying to escape the impending storm.

On the way, Rose made eye contact with one of her dad's best friends, Nate. He was rambling by in his noisy red truck, old-time country music booming from his stereo. Nate waved hello to Rose with a sideways grin, and she sheepishly smiled back.

"So, do you want to come over for dinner?" Kenai asked, as they hurried home side-by-side.

"Oh, that's okay. Thanks, though."

"You sure?" Kenai urged.

"Yeah, I'm sure. Tell your mom I said sorry, but maybe another time."

Rose returned home with a million ideas swimming around her brain. She wanted, needed, to learn more about this Lady Bountiful. Where did she come from? What happened to her? What did Manu mean about time? How could you be in more than one place in one moment?

She made herself some pasta and tomato sauce, and ate it in front of the TV, sitting stationary next to her mom. Rose couldn't follow any of the storyline on the screen; her mind was too focused on the day's events, and Kenai. Was that boy for real? How could any boy be so sweet and smart and handsome at the same time? What would happen this school year?

Would they ever be able to hang out?

After finishing her early dinner, Rose slipped away into her bedroom. She picked up an astrophysics book that she had found on one of her mother's bookshelves. Her mom had hundreds, maybe thousands of books, all stacked on three bookshelves in her bedroom and several more along the hallway walls. Books were the only things that her mom collected, the only material things that seemed to have any worth at all to her.

What was it about time that was so confusing, Rose asked herself. Time was time, wasn't it? We could measure it, count it, depend on it? It always went forward, right? Why, then, did George Eliot say science, which always progressed, could go backwards and forwards? How could Manu be in the past at the same time he was in the present? How come no one ever talked to her about these possibilities before?

Rose finally passed out with the textbook resting securely on her plump belly; it was opened to a chapter about black holes.

*H*ours later, but what felt to her as just minutes, Rose shuddered awake when her door flung open. It was her dad, standing in the doorway, red-faced, one hand holding steady onto the belt around his waist, the other onto the brass doorknob.

"Rose!" he screamed. "Just who were you biking around with this afternoon?"

She didn't know whether to run, crawl into the corner, or stay put. Something deep inside of her told her to stay put.

"Answer me, Rose! Answer me!" he screamed even louder.

"What are you doing, Joe?" her mother screamed back. "What is this all about?" Her mom stood in front of him, blocking Rose from his view.

"Get out of my way, woman!"

"I will not. You tell me, now, what is this all about?"

"Nate told me he saw Rose hanging out with that African boy," Joe barked back. He unbuckled his belt, and began pulling it out from the belt holes.

"So?" Her mom did not budge.

"So? It's bad enough we have all these Mexicans stealing our jobs," he ranted.

"They're not stealing your jobs! They know how to work hard and make sacrifices, not like you lazy, privileged white boys!"

"Now you've really gone too far, Susie!" Joe yelled, moving towards her with his belt out-stretched between his two hands.

"You put that belt away! You have no right!" Her mom reached for the belt.

"No right? She's my daughter, and I don't want her seen with that-"

"That what, Joe? What, Joe? That nice boy? Nicer and smarter than you'll ever be! You're drunk, Joe. Get out of Rose's room and out of this house until you sober up," she said.

"I'm not drunk," her father said, slurring his words.

"No? No? I can smell it on you a mile away! Get out of here, or I'll call the sheriff," she said sternly.

"The sheriff's an hour away from here," he argued.

"Joe, I've had enough of you! Enough of you, Joe! How dare you come into my daughter's-"

"Our daughter's! She's my daughter, too!" he yelled back.

"Well, you have no right to be scaring her with your belt. I thought you promised to never touch her, the way your dad beat you. Joe, you disgust me," she said to him, one hand on her hip, the other pointing a finger at him. He grabbed her finger to lower it.

Rose watched the entire scene huddled on her floor with her arms wrapped around her legs, shoved up against the back of her bed, as if watching a horror movie. She was frightened, but also removed.

Joe grabbed Susie's shirt with both hands when Susie abruptly pushed him off and away from her. He went to slap her face, but she caught his hand, and pushed it downwards. He quickly grabbed Susie's upper arm with his other hand and pulled her into the living room.

"You stay put," Susie yelled to Rose, her head twisted around in Rose's direction as she entered the living room. "Don't move, you hear?" she yelled again to Rose, who was still huddled in her bedroom. "And shut your door!"

Rose watched Susie wrangle herself from her husband's tight grip, pushing him off of her again with both hands.

Rose obeyed her mom's command, shutting her door and locking it, while her mom and dad finished their argument in the living room. Rose placed her left ear against the door so she could hear what they were saying.

"I never would have hit her, Susie! I just wanted to scare her," he pleaded.

"I don't believe you," her mom screamed back. "I don't believe you, and even if I did, why try to scare her like that? What the hell is wrong with you?"

Rose could hear her father's yelling recede; he was begging her mom now, he was saying he was sorry, making the excuse that he was drunk, but that it was also her mom's fault that things had gotten out of hand so quickly. Susie insisted that he leave immediately then Joe started calling her mom a host of bad names, cruel and nasty names that pierced Rose's heart each time another one shot out of his mouth, but soon enough Rose heard the screen and front door slam shut and lock, and knew that her mom had won.

Rose heard her dad's truck zoom away at the same time as she heard her mother burst into tears. Rose left her safe space, unlocking her bedroom door and entering the living room.

"Mom, mom," she kneeled down on the rug, where her mom was holding onto her knees, rocking back and forth. "It's going to be okay, okay? He'll come back, he will." Rose tried to assure her.

"I don't want him to come back, I never want to see him again. Why would you?"

Then her mom cried even louder, and held Rose tighter than she had in a very long time. They held each other like when Rose was younger.

An unexpected happiness engulfed Rose; she was her mommy's little girl again, and it felt so nice, so very nice to be loved for being her, to feel protected, to feel like she mattered. It made the whole scene worth it. She never thought her dad would really hurt her, not physically at least; he had threatened her with the belt plenty of times before, but she would always hide under her bed, and that would be the end of it.

"Why does he hate Kenai so much? I don't understand, Mommy." Rose asked almost inaudibly.

"It's stupid, and he doesn't hate him, really. He doesn't even know him. It's just a good excuse to hate, to be angry at someone else besides himself. But it's himself who he hates, baby. You know that, don't you? It's himself, nobody else. You remember that, okay?"

"I will, Mommy," Rose answered. "But why does he hate himself so much?"

"Because of that ugly war he fought in," Susie said.

"But what does that have to do with-" Rose began.

"Not now," Susie said. "I just can't get into all that now."

After a few minutes, Rose confessed. "Because I love Kenai, Mom, I think I do at least, and I can't not see him, I just can't." Rose began to cry, big, fat rolling tears, so fast her breath couldn't keep up.

"I know, honey," her mom reassured her. "I promise I will always protect you, okay? Don't you worry about anything anymore."

The intensity of the situation brought Susie back to her real self, where she was able to focus on Rose in a way she usually couldn't.

The two of them moved to the couch. Susie patted her lap, signaling Rose to lay down her head. Rose lay down, and Susie brushed her daughter's long, straight dirty blonde hair between her fingers. She kept brushing Rose's hair until Rose was nearly asleep.

Susie carried Rose to her bedroom, and tucked the covers around her. She found the astrophysics book there and grinned. She rested the book just where it had been left opened, on the side table, and then kissed Rose on the forehead.

"I love you, Mommy," Rose whispered.

"I love you more," her mom whispered back. Susie moved to the door, gingerly closing it while never taking her eyes off Rose until the door was completely shut.

Rose could hear the shower start, and was grateful that her mom hadn't indulged in her usual self-pity rant about how she was stuck in her marriage and stuck in Colorado, which allowed Rose to fall asleep soon after she found a comfortable position under the heavy covers.

*R*ose awoke suddenly when she heard her dad's truck roll into the driveway. She looked at the digital clock next to her bed; it was two o'clock in the morning. Rose heard her dad grab something from the refrigerator, most likely the orange juice, and turn on the living room television. She could tell it was one of those action movies, one that he'd seen about twenty to thirty times already. For some reason the violence and murder on the screen often calmed him into a solid slumber.

When the snoring began, she knew her dad had fallen asleep on the couch, and that they had all survived a horrendous, life-altering night. She had no idea what tomorrow would bring, but at least there would be a tomorrow, and that gave her solace enough to close her eyes, too, and dream.

Rose awoke to utter silence and dressed quietly in her room, throwing a T-shirt and shorts on over a bathing suit. She brushed her teeth and washed her face, in a quiet so vast she could hear the clock ticking and herself breathing in it.

When she entered the living room, her mother and father were sitting like statues at the kitchen table as if their entire existence depended on waiting for Rose's presence.

Rose couldn't remember the last time she saw them up this early together, sharing breakfast. Normally her father was gone by six, and her mother slept until ten.

"I'm sorry for last night," her father said as sweetly as he could.

"It's okay," Rose said, lowering her head.

She quickly grabbed a banana from the fruit bowl and headed towards the door. She wanted to tell him that she wasn't going to stop hanging out with Kenai, but she didn't want to get them both upset. She ran out the front door before they could ask where she was going, before they could say anything at all to her. In the distance she heard her mom yell, "Rose, Rose," but she tuned it out, and ran ever faster towards her favorite place.

It was a hot and unusually humid day. A couple of deer danced out of her way as they crossed the road, headed for the river. Perched on the next-door neighbor's wood fence, a handful of black-capped chickadees were talking among themselves while a red-tailed hawk flew overhead. The chokecherry trees announced their ripening with dark red berries bursting in long, skinny bundles; dogwoods showed off their white berries, and wild raspberries called out for picking. Hummingbirds hovered over Colorado blue columbines, and swarms of bees hummed around Alpine sunflowers.

All the signs of late August, including the dry river rocks exposed several feet into the riverbed, were abundant. A perfect day to go to the river beach. When Rose arrived, she found Kenai already there. He was balancing on the stones, making his way to the end where a pine tree had fallen from a lightning storm last summer. No one had removed the heavy, dead tree even though it covered up most of the black sand. Less people visited there now as a result.

"Hey!" Kenai shouted out to Rose, cupping his hands around his mouth to project his call. "Thought I'd find you here. I can't believe how hot it is already."

"I know," she said less enthusiastically, and breathless.

She walked past Kenai, and treaded heavily to the river's edge. She sat down in a humpf, and started digging up the rich, wet sand in her hands and painting the rocks with it.

"Whaddya doing?" he asked her.

"What does it look like I'm doing?" she said sarcastically, her face looking down at some grey shells.

"Hey, what's the matter?" he asked, close enough now to see the heaviness in her eyes.

"Nothing. Just a little tired today. I just want to play with the mud, is that okay? I'm not in the mood to talk to Manu, okay?"

"Okay," Kenai said. "Are you in the mood to talk to me?"

"Not really, I mean, I don't really feel like talking to anyone, but you can sit with me if you want."

So Kenai sat next to Rose, glooping the dark mud through his hands, and building it up over his legs. Rose coated the rocks with the mud, then grabbed a stick and drew some triangles. Kenai piled the mud until it became a volcano then planted a flag-branch at the top, while Rose balanced flat rocks into a mini-sculpture. The sun beat heavy on their backs. Rose took off her shirt and shorts to reveal her purple one-piece bathing suit;

Kenai took off his pink polo shirt. He splashed her, and she splashed him back.

Earlier in the summer, they could fully immerse themselves in the water, but today it stopped at their hips. She splashed in right behind him, and pushed water at his chest. He did the same.

"First one in the water-" he said teasing Rose, and jumped into the swimming hole to their left. They let the current pull them around the bend to the stiller waters. Soon enough, the two of them were laughing, and cooling off in the tamed tributary, submerging like eels under the low tide. A rainbow trout wiggled beside them, while a pair of electric blue dragonflies buzzed on a floating log, mating. Water strider bugs rowed near the pine tree's thick, dead roots. And just upstream from them, beavers had started building a dam.

Almost cold, the children ran out of the river, and rested towel-less on the pebbly bank, their backs and legs nestled into the cool sand. The piercing sunrays eased their goose bumps, and evaporated their wetness, warming them towards one another.

"I don't know why my mom hates living here," Rose said aloud. "This is heaven."

The two of them pondered that idea for some time, and let their thoughts travel in and out of their bodies. Their hands lay palms up to the clear skies, and they each made their own wishes. Soon enough their peace was broken by a large and loud family, bumbling down to the river from the short, bumpy trail that connected the river to the road. Obvious outsiders, the campers were hauling umbrellas, towels, a picnic basket, and a large cooler. Rose moved her hand on top of Kenai's, and without words, they lifted each other up, then balanced on the grey rocks that lead to her special spot, which was now their special spot together. The metallic and elephant-grey rocks made layers around the dried-up river, like giant bubbles in a clay-red soapy bath. Only yards from the invaded beach, they were also worlds away.

"Feeling better?" he asked her.

"Yeah, thanks," she said.

"Wanna talk about it?"

"No, not really," she remarked. "I'm having too much fun now to remember all that."

Manu suddenly appeared. He didn't wait for a song or question or an introduction. He kept on, as if the three of them had never parted.

"*Va benne*, I don't know for sure that he couldn't give her *bambini-*"

"*Bambini?*" Rose asked.

"Babies, children. Lady Bountiful was never with child, and as most of the staff knew that Mr. Osgood's first wife, the Intolerable Irene, had never been with child, they assumed it was Mr. Osgood who could not make it happen."

"What's intolerable? Who was Irene?" Kenai wanted to know.

"They say Irene did not like living in Redstone, in the middle of nowhere. She preferred Glenwood Springs, and spent a lot of time at the Hotel Colorado causing trouble before they kicked her out. Mr. Osgood did not like that one bit."

"I can imagine," Rose said in a very grown-up voice.

"Does that place still exist?" Manu asked.

"What place?" Kenai replied.

"Hotel Colorado," Manu clarified.

"Definitely," Rose replied. "People say it's haunted; they say many of the people who work and stay there have seen and heard ghosts-" She stopped herself suddenly. "I'm sorry, I wasn't thinking, does that offend you?"

"What? That there are other ghosts?"

"Spirits," Kenai corrected.

"Oh, you mean the word 'ghost'"? Manu asked.

"Yeah," Kenai said, slightly embarrassed.

"Spirits, ghosts, ghouls, goblins, those are just words, they make no difference to me," Manu said.

"But words *do* matter," Kenai said.

"Okay," Rose pushed on, avoiding a discussion of semantics. "Does it bother you that people are scared of spirits, that they call it haunted when they experience one, and that most people don't believe in you?"

"No," Manu said, and then paused. "Spirits are real, and unfortunately not all of us are nice. In truth, the ones who stay behind are more angry than sad or confused, and they take it out on others, giving us all a bad reputation."

Manu told the children that it was common knowledge in the town that Irene liked to socialize with the rich and famous. Irene had published some bad romantic poetry and essays, and people said that Mr. Osgood even started a publishing house in New York just so her first romance novel could get published. She liked to travel around America and Europe without Mr. Osgood, and when Mr. Osgood began working on the castle, she ran away with another man, whom she eventually married.

Mr. Osgood had *The New York Times* write an article about how Irene was killed by a runaway horse in Central Park in New York City, but apparently that was a lie. Manu held his hand to his mouth as if telling the children a secret, and started speaking more quietly. Before Irene left him, Manu continued, Mr. Osgood met the next Mrs. Osgood, Alma Regina Shelgrem, at the Palace of King Leopold the Second of Belgium. Mr. Osgood was trying to get money from the king, and instead met the *amore* of his life. He brought her to Denver in 1899, the year he and Irene divorced, but Alma was not received too well in the beginning. Something happened with a friend of hers, and another man in New York City. A man named Arthur. "I think Arthur killed himself - uh-oh," Manu said and then stopped himself.

"What is it, Manu?" Rose asked.

"I forgot for a moment that you two are children. This is all too much for you, isn't it?"

"No, no!" both Rose and Kenai insisted.

"We know a lot, actually, because of the Internet," Rose explained.

"What's the Internet?" Manu asked, leaning in from deep curiosity.

"It's, it's, it's like a big encyclopedia in the sky," Kenai said. "Do you know what an encyclopedia is?"

"Yes, we had the *Encyclopedia Britannica* in our library. But what do you mean 'in the sky?'" Manu asked.

"Well, it's kind of hard to explain, but-," Kenai began to say.

"Did you have phones?" Rose asked Manu.

"Yes, of course," Manu answered. "In the castle."

"Well, you know how you heard someone's voice over the phone? Well, we have machines that send information to one another, like a voice from one phone to another."

"Oh, okay," Manu said, trying to visualize what she was describing. "It sounds very fancy," he said.

"Not really," Kenai said. It's for everyone, really."

"Can we go back to the story now?" Rose asked.

"Okay, if you will tell me more about these information machines later," Manu said as if bargaining.

"I promise," Rose said.

"*Va benne*, where was I now?"

"You were talking about the man from New York who killed himself," Rose said.

Arthur left a note behind that blamed Mrs. Alma for his problems, Manu explained, which was reported in *The New York Times*. When word got to Denver about the scandal, the rich people of Denver rejected Mrs. Alma. According to Manu, she became grateful for the rejection, because it meant she didn't have to bother with any of them. She didn't care much for phonies or rich people, she had had enough of that in Sweden, and that's not why she loved Mr. Osgood, either. It had nothing to do with his money, she had informed Manu. She wanted to help people, and believed the money could help in doing that. She thought that she and Mr. Osgood had a shared vision about how the world could and should be.

"She was a beautiful dreamer, *bellissima*," Manu said as if in a daydream. "I was surprised she wasn't Italian instead of Swedish. She did, however, on many occasions, mention Arthur to me with much despondency in her voice, *voce triste*. I don't think she realized how much she loved him while he was alive. This is all she told me about her past, and I didn't ask her many questions, either. She did tell me, *tuttavia*, that she wanted to write the story of her life, and I did see her on many occasions writing in her journal. She said she was going to bury the journal in Redstone for someone to find in the future, because she didn't want anyone knowing anything about her while she was alive and living here."

"You mean, you think that journal is still buried here?" Kenai and Rose burst with excitement.

"Yes, I do," Manu said. "But I know very little about anything that's happened since my death."

"Why? That's strange, because you are here with us now."

"Because until meeting both of you, I haven't really been interested in learning about anything else."

"So why now? Why are you interested now?" Rose asked.

"I think it has something to do with what's keeping me here. Maybe it's the right time for me to leave, finally, but I'm not sure how. Maybe you two are supposed to help me with this. Maybe you two can help me with this somehow?"

Kenai and Rose beamed at each other. "Of course!" they said almost in unison. "We can figure it out together."

"Where was that spot where you saw her burying the journal?" Kenai asked hurriedly, breaking the eeriness that had taken over their present space. "Maybe it will give us a clue of how to get you to leave? Where do you think it could be?"

"How do you think her journal could help me? I just don't see the connection," Manu said.

"I just have a feeling," Kenai said.

"Maybe we'll read something that will help explain why you are stuck here, or will help you get past Lady Bountiful, maybe there's some kind of hidden message in there for you?" Rose imagined out loud, excited about the possibility of being detectives with Kenai.

"Okay. To make you happy, I will help you with your adventure. Maybe it will help me, too."

Manu took a moment, and then began, "A few times I saw her go down by the river, directly across from Deer Park. But once she left, I never had the courage to see if that's where her journal was. I thought about it, but it felt wrong to me, like I would be betraying her if I actually found it. So, I let it be," Manu explained.

"Do you think we should just go there, in the middle of the night, and start digging?" Rose asked.

"No, no, *mia cara ragazza,* I wouldn't advise it," Manu warned. "You could get in big trouble if someone caught you."

"But there's no other way," Kenai said.

"Why don't you go up there in the daylight and just look around? Have you ever been there?" Manu asked them.

"Once," Kenai said. "On a tour of the castle. Many years ago. I don't remember much. But we certainly didn't go to the river. It seemed a far ways from the castle."

"I've never visited," Rose said, hanging her head. "But I've always wanted to."

"*Mio Dio!* It's like living in New York City and never visiting the Statue of Liberty, " Manu said.

"I have!" Kenai exclaimed. "When we visited New York City last summer. It was crowded and there was a really long line, but it was amazing once we reached the top and looked out over the city."

"Your parents take you to do so many cool things," Rose said enviously. "You're so lucky."

"Your parents are your real parents," Kenai said defensively.

"Now, now, kids," Manu said. "*Silencio.* No need to fight here. We all have easy and hard, fun and not-so-fun parts of our lives; don't compare yourself to someone else that way. It's silly, and a waste of time. You chose your parents before you were born, to learn something that you needed to learn. Now, even if you don't remember why or how you chose them, it's your job to figure out what you came back to Earth to learn."

"Is that true? Is that really true?" Kenai asked, doubting Manu for the first time ever.

"It's not my job to convince you, Kenai, but your job to find out for yourself."

Rose stared off into space. Whether or not it was true, and she always believed in the possibility of anything, it was a nice thought, and one that made her feel better about, well, everything. We all have our own beliefs that either make us feel better or worse, she thought, so why not choose to believe in something that makes us feel better, and doesn't hurt other people at the same time?

"In any case," Rose said, "I would like to go on the castle tour. We could go this weekend, before school starts. It would be fun, and I have some money left over from the money I won at the art show."

"You won money from an art show?" Kenai asked.

"It's no big deal," Rose said. "Just something from school. It was just an abstract design. I'm no good at drawing something real, but I like making designs."

"Cool," Kenai said. "Very cool."

"So, it's settled then," Manu confirmed. "The two of you will go on a tour of the castle, and then you will tell me all about it."

"Can't you join us?" Rose asked.

"You two go alone, just to be safe. *Per favore*," Manu said as if exhausted. "I don't want to bump into anyone else who could possibly sense me."

And then he vanished, as if scared of his own shadow.

Rose and Kenai dipped their feet into the shallow water, splashing each other's long legs, ecstatic about their new adventure, leaning their heads back to absorb every last drop of warm summer sunshine that beamed down on their glorious faces. The bliss Rose felt bubbling up inside made her forget her mom and dad and their fight entirely, that is, until it was time to go back home.

10

When Rose returned to her house later in the afternoon, she found Mechau curled up on the porch. She knelt down to pat his head until he meandered off. She opened her front door inch by inch to find her mom sitting at the kitchen table. Her mom was doing a crossword puzzle in the local paper. Rose headed directly for her room.

"Hey, Rose, I have to tell you something," Susie said.

"What is it?" Rose asked without turning around.

"Please sit down, Rosie. I need to talk to you."

Rose sidled over to the chair across from her mom. She sat turned away from the table.

"Please look at me, Rosie," her mom said, pleading.

Rose moved her body a smidge without committing her full

attention to her mom.

"Your dad's left," Susie said to Rose.

Rose finally looked at her mom, and a wave of anger burst from her chest up through her throat.

"What do you mean? Where's he gone?" Rose barked.

"Home," her mom replied, patient with Rose's ugly tone.

"Home? Isn't this his home?" Rose asked, puzzled.

"To Atlanta, to stay with Grandpa and YaYa," Susie clarified. "Grandpa's got some work for your dad to do, and we both thought it was perfect timing for us to take a little break, you know, after last night and all."

"Are you getting divorced?" Rose asked pointedly, tears building up in the corners of her eyes.

"We just need a break from each other, Rosie, for just a little while, you know. And it's not like there's so much work out here for Dad, anyway."

"When's he coming back?"

"In a month or two. He's not sure how long the job will take. He wanted to say goodbye to you, he really did, but he thought he'd get too emotional, and it was just easier for him to leave as soon as the decision was made," Susie explained.

"Easier for who? For both of you? How about me? It's not easier for me!" Rose exclaimed.

"I'm sorry, honey, but things are going to get better, okay?" her mom said with a stronger voice. "They will, I promise. We just need some time. This will be good. I'm going to look for a job-" Susie began.

"Doing what?" Rose said condescendingly.

"Stop being rude, Rosie. I'm ready. It's time."

"Can I be excused?" Rose demanded.

"Sure, of course," Susie said. "I love you, honey. Your dad is going to call you later tonight, from the road, okay?"

"Fine. I don't care," she said, and stomped off to her bedroom. Rose was actually a little relieved that her dad would be gone for a while, even if she didn't want to admit that to her mom. He had scared her, and she didn't want that to happen again, for him to hurt her mom. But at the same time, she loved her dad and didn't want him to disappear for too long.

Rose whipped out her pastels and sketchpad, and smeared the page with black and grey and red shapes. She wiped away her tears with her forearms. She was crying hard now, more out of confusion than anything else.

She turned on the local radio station. There was a program on featuring blues music, exactly what she wanted to listen to at that moment. Why can't they just get along? she cried to herself. She obsessed over this question so much, she felt compelled to ask her mom. She returned to the kitchen table, her arms crossed over her chest, standing in front of where her mom was still doing the crossword puzzle.

"I just have one question, Mom," Rose said. "Why can't you two get along? What's so hard about it?"

"As we get older our differences are becoming much bigger. When we met, our differences were exciting, it's what attracted us to each other, and now our differences are what's driving us apart," her mom answered, looking directly into Rose's eyes.

"But now you have me in common. Isn't that enough to make you the same?"

"I hope so," Susie responded. "That's what we're praying for. Because we both love you so much, we want to do what's best for you."

Rose retreated back to her room and her art. She wanted her parents to be happy, and she also wanted them to stay together. The hardest part was that she felt she couldn't do anything about it, either way, and that it was partly her fault somehow, although she couldn't figure out how, or what, to do to make it better.

11

*R*ose and Kenai biked up the aristocratic road that led up to the Redstone Castle. They passed Rose's dad's favorite fishing bank on the right moving into a more forested section of the river's edge that nestled around the handful of houses aligning the dirt road, including the Swiss chalet gamekeeper's timber lodge. The road opened to a white pedestal gatehouse welcoming visitors to the mansion as a lighthouse called in its sailors. They parked their bikes in a lot to the right of the pastel green, white-outlined, mahogany red-roofed castle.

They all gathered outside of the courtyard, awaiting their tour guide, Patricia. She was dressed in the fashion of the time, a long, heavy cloth dress with an ornate velvet hat made of flowers, silver beads, and lace. The peach-colored dress came in tight at the middle, but fluffy in the skirt and arms, then tight again at the neck. The embroidered lines of lace ran around the dress's top and down the arms, making circles near the hem and wrists. Patricia wore black, laced boots and used a white and purple parasol as a cane. She looked marvelous, and played the part perfectly. She walked over to Rose and Kenai.

"Any reason you're here on your own?" she asked them.

"Yes," Rose answered, not sure how Patricia would interpret her answer.

"We were just curious about the castle," Kenai said. "Rose has never been here. I have, with my parents, a couple years ago, but her parents, well, um, we just thought it would be fun to come here together."

"Well, if at any time you get bored, you can wander off and look around the castle yourself," she said. "But please do it discretely so that no one else notices. I can't have everyone else doing that."

"Oh my goodness!" Kenai exclaimed. "Thank you so much!"

"Yes, thank you!" Rose exclaimed, too.

"It's my pleasure," Patricia said. "Lady Bountiful loved children. She would show you around the castle herself if she could!"

Patricia led the group into the courtyard where one of Osgood's two-seat carriages butted against the tall, wide doors that were large enough for horses to trespass through. Standing near the carriage, Patricia began the tour by recounting the story about one of Osgood's electric cars:

"One of Osgood's guests teased him that his 1904 Pope Winton electric car could never get to the top of McClure Pass at 8,775 feet. We are at 7,200 feet here in Redstone. The next morning on the guests' horseback trip towards the Elk Mountain Range, they found Osgood's car in a clearing at the very top of the pass. Legend has it that the car didn't really make it to the top, but that Osgood made some of his employees take apart the car, carry it up the pass, and reassemble it there."

When she was finished with the story, Patricia moved the group to the other side of the front courtyard, and stood beside the dragon fountain. She explained that the fountain, which was used to spit water into a marble trough just a couple of feet ahead of it, was a gift to Osgood from the Yule Marble Company. The trough was heavy enough to require a special wagon to haul it from its origin in Marble, twelve miles up the Crystal River. That marble quarry provided stone for many noted American buildings and monuments, including the Denver State Capitol, the Lincoln Memorial and the Tomb of the Unknown Soldier in Washington, DC, the City Hall in San Francisco, and the New York Municipal and Equitable Buildings in New York City. There was a very interesting history of Marble and its quarry, but she wouldn't have time to recount it to them; they would have to go visit Marble themselves for that.

She went on to say that the house sat on 4,200 acres, and that its style was borrowed from English Tudor manors. The adjacent red cliff provided the exterior stone for the 25,000 square foot building, which was designed by a Denver architect named Theodore Boal. There were forty-two rooms and eight bathrooms, fourteen fireplaces, all with indoor plumbing and electricity, a true accomplishment in those days. Rose especially loved the bold turret, which protruded so elegantly from the front of the house. Only five of the rooms were for guests, as the Osgoods preferred entertaining smaller groups, while ten rooms on the back side of the house were designated for servants, valets and the watchman.

The children wondered whether Manu had ever slept in any of those rooms, or if any of them had indeed once been his.

They entered the mansion by a thick wood door lavished with flowery ironwork to protect the high glass window. A taxidermy ram's head rested above the frame. They all gathered near the wooden staircase. As they eased their way around the group, the children peeked into the living room, otherwise known as the Great Hall. The walls were white, with etched wood wainscoting. Metal encased chandeliers lit by large yellow orbs hung from the ceiling; velvet drapes announced the windows looking down onto the meadow, and two electric blue lounge chairs mirrored each other on top of a patterned rug. There were a few decorations: paintings, vases, candelabra lamps; but it was the baby grand piano in the corner that struck Kenai. He felt an urge to go over and play it, but of course kept his distance.

Patricia led the group into the living room, while Kenai moved closer to the piano. He could feel vibrations there, and hear music emanating from the keys. He noticed the sheet music on the piano ledge was entitled *The Redstone Waltz* and had Alma Osgood's name written on the top, naming her as the composer.

They soon moved into the dining room with its long, wooden table and attached sun porch. Patricia explained how the Osgoods entertained all sorts of dignitaries, including Theodore Roosevelt, John D. Rockefeller. Sr. and Jr., JP Morgan, and King Leopold II of Belgium, the man who had made their meeting possible. The Osgoods had spent a considerable amount of time traveling throughout Europe, buying furniture and décor for their mansion.

The library was the most elaborate of the rooms, which made perfect sense to the children, based on the story Manu told them about the George Eliot book. It must have been Mr. Osgood's homage to his bright and beautiful wife, who not only read voraciously, but was also an outstanding horsewoman, hunter and composer. The ceilings were etched with gold-inlaid leather, and the walls were made of oak, blocked off from the Great Hall by a hunter green velvet curtain hung by gold rings. The light sconces resembled leaves and the chairs ranged from stiff, art deco wood structures to plush aquamarine couches. Tiffany lamps and Stickley chairs, prominent items in their day, could be identified throughout the house.

The tour group followed Patricia up to the second floor, where all the walls were lined with yellow linen wallpaper stenciled with pineapples, "the universal sign of welcome and hospitality," Patricia informed the group.

Alma's bedroom was of greatest interest to the children, as they imagined her lying sick in bed with Manu reading to her from the night table's embroidered chair. They longed to open any drawer they could find, and awaited the opportunity to let the group go ahead of them. As they sneaked over to one of her bureaus, an older woman from the tour scolded them, discouraging them from searching any more. They wanted to tell her that Patricia said it would be okay for them to explore, but then remembered how Patricia told them to be discrete. They'd have to be more careful and detective-like if they were going to discover anything. The chances were infinitesimal that there would be anything left behind. Even though seventy-five percent of the furniture was the same as it was back then, the castle had turned hands many times, recently posing as a bed and breakfast.

The children headed downstairs to the main floor again, and then to the basement. Rose and Kenai both shuddered as they made their way down the stairs.

"Do you smell that?" Rose whispered to Kenai.

"Yeah, what is that?"

"Smells like cigar to me," Rose said.

"Really? I don't even know what that smells like," Kenai admitted.

"Yeah, my dad sometimes smokes cigars on our patio. I've caught him a bunch of times. He never smokes in the house, though, like my mom does, so that's good. My mom doesn't smoke cigars, only cigarettes." Rose wasn't sure if she had said too much to Kenai. She was embarrassed that her parents smoked, but was reassured when Kenai didn't make a face or comment when she revealed her secret.

As they turned the corner to enter the game room, the children immediately spotted the same person: a short, chubby, middle-aged man in a three-piece checkered suit with gold loops hanging from both sides of the middle vest button to beneath the blazer, a proper tan hat, a bushy, long mustache that curled up at the edges, a strong chin, piercing eyes with raised eyebrows, a receding hairline, and a cigar in his mouth. He was pacing the room between the fireplace and the knight statue in the not-so shining armor. The room was dark and dank, with a poker table, pool table and dartboard filling the space. Rose felt the coldness of the stone, and the coldness of her own hands. Patricia continued talking; it was clear that no one else was seeing what they were seeing: the spirit of John Cleveland Osgood.

It seemed to them that Mr. Osgood could not see them, or that he was simply not interested in them. He was pacing and uttering random words and sentences to himself. Often he said, "Alma, Alma, my dear Alma, where have you gone?" But then he would start talking about business, the railroads and the coal mines, and Rockefeller and Gould, and Jerome, Kebler, and Cass, and the unions, "the unions, the unions, damn the unions," and shaking his head, mumbling, "What went wrong, Dr. Corwin?" His voice was so strong they could hardly hear Patricia's anymore.

Step by step the children moved closer to Mr. Osgood, but he could still not see them. A couple of times, he walked right through them as a chill ran up and down their bodies. They were close enough, however, to hear one of his longer diatribes:

"The strong financial interests which have acquired control of the stock of the company and have assumed its management, and who will give it the financial backing which is necessary to the full development of its properties, have treated me with the utmost consideration and fairness and at no time has there been the slightest friction or antagonism between myself and the new interests. I can state positively that it is not the desire of these interests to change the character of the corporation as a distinctively Colorado enterprise, and that the business will be managed by residents of Colorado-"

The children had no idea what this mumbo-jumbo meant, but they listened nonetheless. They thought Mr. Osgood almost sounded like background noise from the news on TV.

"You see, I was good, I was good, Kebler, I was a good man, Alma," Osgood whined as he paced and smoked his cigar. "Listen, here," he kept on, as if talking to Kebler and Mrs. Osgood directly. He looked down on the pool table, as if reading from something line-by-line, "Read here in *The Denver Times* what they say about my Ruby of the Rockies, about my dear Ruby, my Redstone." He quoted: "The great reservoir of the Colorado Iron and Fuel company-" then paused and looked up again. "They got that wrong, see, it's Colorado Fuel and Iron, but that's why they're *The Denver Times* and not *The New York Times*," he chuckled to himself.

He continued, "Redstone was finished this week and the electric lights were turned on Wednesday. Redstone is now assuming metropolitan airs. I like that," he said, "metropolitan airs. Not bad, not bad at all." He kept reading aloud: "When one comes to think of it all, it seems simply wonderful…Simply wonderful!" Osgood repeated triumphantly.

He continued reading the newspaper article, "On this spot but a few short years ago the wolf howled and the coyote skulked; the elk, the deer, the bear, the mountain lion and other wild animals roamed undisturbed by the presence of man. It was a solitude. Now it is a hive of industry, a thrifty mountain town emerging from its swaddling clothes with a future. All is activity, and the modern electric light turns night into day.

"Oh, I love this reporter! He is a goddamn poet, a poet, I say! We must find him and have him write for us exclusively!" Osgood exclaimed, joyful and exuberant, but in a flash, his mood changed, and he was back to justifying himself: "Even *The New York Times*, nineteen months later wrote this about us: Fifteen months ago Redstone consisted of little outside of some rude huts or 'dug-outs,' to use the more expressive Western vernacular. Today it is the most beautiful town in Colorado. A-ha, you hear that? The most beautiful town in Colorado, the most beautiful town in Colorado!'"

Osgood quickened his pace, covering his face with his hands then lifted his head, shaking it all the while. Then he put his hands in his pocket, and looked out the window. "Look at my deer and my elk, my animals, my zoo, they miss us, too, dear, they miss us. Won't you come back?"

Patricia noticed the children in the corner, their mouths wide open, yet not looking at her. She knew she couldn't see what they were seeing, even though she suspected they were seeing something supernatural, but said nothing of it. She raised the volume of her voice though to get their attention, which it did. She went on with her tale: "…and so it was, that Mr. Osgood had him shot, right here in this very room."

The children could not believe they had missed the beginning of this shocking story, and now they were too embarrassed to ask her to tell it again. They stored the fact in their memories; maybe Manu would know what Patricia was talking about. The rest of the tour group seemed too entranced to ask any questions.

Rose and Kenai followed the group out of the game room. They had their fill of Mr. Osgood for now. As they climbed back upstairs, several spirits dressed in servant uniforms passed them by. Behind them, a handful of spirit laborers and their wives followed suit. They seemed to be listening to Osgood yell at them, "Go away, you damn people! Just go away already!" And so the parade of spirits turned about, and made their way to the top of the stairs alongside Kenai and Rose. They floated into the air, their sweet-smelling, warm breezes kissing Kenai and Rose's bare arms and necks; cooler air and goose-bumps on Rose and Kenai's arms and legs replaced the air of spirits once they were dutifully gone. Rose and Kenai were left at the front door to exit the castle with the rest of the tour group. It was then that they realized they had come unprepared, without a notepad or camera. All they had in their possession in which to recall their jointly haunted experience were their memories. As they headed for their bikes, Patricia approached them.

"Hey kids, what was it you saw down there in the game room?"

Kenai and Rose gazed into each other's eyes.

"Nothing, nothing," they both chanted.

"Nothing? Are you sure about that?" she asked, fidgeting with the metal rings on her fingers.

"We're sure," they said in unison.

"Okay, well, if you ever want to tell me, I'd love to hear. I know the castle is haunted. I just can't see them, you know, but maybe you two can?"

"Uh-huh," they replied coyly.

"Thanks for the tour. It was great," Rose added.

"Well, I did see a ghost once," Patricia admitted. "It was a woman with a beehive hairdo. She was sitting at the dining room table. When I turned around and looked again, she was gone. But that's the only ghost I ever saw, even though I think there are a lot more around here. I'm not sure it was Alma, but I'm pretty sure it was. I've also smelled Mr. Osgood's cigar in the basement many times. Well, I'm glad you liked the tour. If you have other questions, feel free to get in touch with me."

She pulled a stack of business cards from a hidden pocket and handed one to each of them. "I'd really love to hear from you," she said.

She turned around, back into the castle's heavy front door. The hem of her elaborate dress nearly got caught while the door was closing behind her.

"Do you think we should tell her?" Rose said under her breath as they approached their bikes. "Maybe she'd tell us something more. Things she normally doesn't tell the group," she said, buckling her bike helmet.

"What do you want to know?" Kenai asked.

"About the guy Osgood shot," Rose said.

"Well, let's talk to Manu about it," Kenai answered, placing his bike helmet on his head.

"Do you think she'd know about the journal?" Rose asked.

"I say we figure it out a little more first," Kenai said.

"Good idea," Rose said, and then waited a moment to ask Kenai. "Did you see all those other spirits? Walking around, with Osgood yelling at them?"

"Yes," he said. "I saw, I heard them, too."

"I thought so," Rose said. "But why do you think all those spirits hang around there, when they're still being treated so badly?"

"Maybe they don't know they're dead," Kenai surmised. "Maybe they think they deserve to always be treated that way."

"It's so sad to think that even after dying they're still being treated so badly," Rose said.

"I know," Kenai said. "I think it must be hard to stop thinking of yourself in a certain way when you've lived like that your whole life, you know?"

"So true," Rose said. "But it's still sad."

The children contemplated going down to the river and searching for the journal, but then decided against it. They had had enough for the day.

"Race you to the bottom of the hill," Kenai said, pointing to the road that headed for Redstone, not towards the river directly below the castle. All the visitors from the tour had already left the castle. By the time they reached the gatehouse, just a few hundred feet from the parking lot, they were riding side by side and had forgotten all about the competition of making it to the bottom first.

Eyes and minds wide open, they let the wind carry them to the next leg of their journey. It was just past three o'clock, the hottest time of the day, and the best time of day for ice cream.

12

Rose awoke to rustling sounds outside her window. The morning breeze was colder; various tips of the quaking aspen leaves had already turned yellow. She pulled her orange-flowered drapes back to find a large, mother bear with two small cubs walking across her backyard. The mother was picking at and feeding herself from the branches and bushes, while her babies followed close behind. The cubs looked small enough to still be of nursing age; their delight, then, in the fresh grasses, honey and insects, roots and flowers, acorns and berries, and occasional meat, would only come through their mother's milk.

As the summer was ending, the bears had less and less to forage up in the mountains; they were starting their feast for hibernation, bulking up for the long, bitter months ahead of them.

Throughout the autumn season, a bear could gain one-and-a-half pounds each day to store enough fat for winter torpor, a period of two hundred days when they go without food.

On this cloudy late morning, a week before school started, Kenai knocked on Rose's door and asked her if she wanted to go to Glenwood Springs with him and his dad. Rose turned to her mom, who was sitting at the kitchen table with the Help Wanted section open.

"Can I?" she asked.

"I don't see why not. Where in Glenwood Springs?"

"The Caverns Adventure Park," Kenai answered, his head peeking into the house.

"That's too expensive for us!" Susie said immediately.

"Oh, but my dad got some free passes and my mom said she'd stay home with my sister, so, Rose can come?"

"Okay, then, just have her back by dark, alright?" She paused for a moment then added, "That's very nice of you, Kenai. Thank you."

"No problem," Kenai said. Rose's heart was bursting out of her chest. She had never gone anywhere outside of Redstone with Kenai. And she had never been to the caverns. Now she was going. And with Kenai. This was turning out to be the best summer of her life, by far.

"Let me just get ready," Rose said. "I'll be quick. You can wait here if you want, or I can meet you at your house, or-" Rose stammered. She could hardly believe this was actually happening.

"I'll wait," he said.

"You can come inside," Susie's mom said.

"It's alright. I'm fine here," Kenai answered.

"Come in!" Rose said, feeling freer with her dad far away. "You two," referring to her mom and Kenai, "can get to know each other while I, I, you know-" she started to say and then ran into her room before she made an even greater fool of herself.

Susie and Kenai made small talk about the weather as Rose grabbed a few things for her backpack: a camera she got two birthdays ago, a notepad and a few pens, a slicker in case it rained, and a handful of coins and dollar bills she had collected in a glass jar over the past couple of months. She slung the backpack over her shoulder.

As she and Kenai were leaving her house, her mom casually handed her a twenty-dollar bill.

"Thanks, Mom," Rose said, but not too excitedly. She didn't want Kenai to think that it was such a big deal for her mom to give her so much money even though it was.

"Bye, Mrs. Engle!"

"Call me Susie," she replied.

"Okay," he said, without naming her this time. "Thanks for letting Rose go," he said under his breath as they headed out the front door.

The two children walked hand-in-hand to Kenai's house, where his dad was waiting on the porch. He was wearing a hooded college sweatshirt, jeans and worn-in sneakers. He looked much younger than her parents with his bright green eyes and tiny freckles around his nose.

"Are we ready?" his dad asked.

"Yup," Kenai said.

"Thanks so much for inviting me, Mr. Lurie," Rose said.

"Lonn," he corrected her, brushing a strand of curly, auburn hair from his forehead.

"Thank you, Lonn," she said. "I've never been to the caverns before."

"Well, I'm glad we could be the ones to take you," he said. "We haven't been there since we brought Desta home, so it will be fun for us, too. I think they've added some new features. She's still too small to join us, though."

The three of them made it to the caverns in forty-five minutes. Lonn handed the cashier at the Iron Mountain Station the complimentary tickets and made reservations for a cave tour. They proceeded to the tram. With six seats available, they had to share the ride in the gondola with another couple visiting from Denver. Half-way up the mountain, they could see the Alpine Coaster's silver tracks, and decided that's what they wanted to do first.

Even though the sky was still overcast, the stunning panoramic view of the Rocky Mountains made them all happy and calm. The gondola made a sudden stop, and swayed back and forth for about a minute. Everyone made silly jokes to deal with the delay.

When they finally reached the top, they had to enter the park through the gift shop. Lonn moved them along, and soon they were sprinting to the Alpine Coaster ride. The children flew down the mountain, each in their own car. The ride was over in a nanosecond, or so it felt, and then they headed for the Giant Canyon Swing. Lonn followed behind them, more like a shadow than a chaperone.

Rose and Kenai dared each other to go on the swing; it soared like a pendulum 1,300 feet over the Glenwood Canyons and the town of Glenwood Springs at almost fifty miles per hour. Rose never thought she would ever have the courage to go on that kind of thrill ride, but with Kenai by her side, somehow she felt anything was possible.

"Are you sure you want to do this?" she asked him.

"No, but we should do it anyway," Kenai said.

"You'll be proud of yourselves after you do it," Lonn chimed in. "And it's a lot of fun!"

"C'mon," Kenai said.

"Okay, okay," Rose said, and after a short wait on line, they were strapped in tight. Before they could change their minds, the swing took off, back and forth, back and forth, farther and farther over the cliff; they linked their arms around one another, squeezing firmer and firmer like a tourniquet, so anxious they could hardly catch a breath. Rose had heard it was scarier to look down, so she looked up to the sky. Kenai had heard the opposite, and so kept his gaze downward. They screamed louder and louder, until the ride began its slowdown. Once they realized they were safe, they began to giggle and tease each other. They took deep breaths when the engineer removed their straps, and jumped off like Olympic sprinters at the starting line. They stood squarely on the ground, grateful that there was ground to stand on.

"Good job, you two," Lonn said, congratulating them. "We have about an hour until the cave tour. Now that your stomachs are upside down, should we get some lunch?"

"Yes!" Kenai exclaimed. They walked back to the entrance of the park to eat on the restaurant deck. Rose wanted to get a cheeseburger, but Kenai and Lonn, both vegetarians, got salads and fruit plates, so Rose did also. Even though she tried to pay for her meal, Lonn insisted on treating.

"You guys having a good time?" Lonn asked them.

"The best time," Rose said. "It's strange, I feel like since we left Redstone, hardly any time has gone by at all, but I know it has."

"It's like time isn't really timed," Kenai added.

"What do you mean by that, Kee?" Lonn asked.

"I mean, I know we measure time in seconds and minutes,

but it's like there's another time, a time that we can't measure. Like, when I'm doing something I like doing, time goes faster, and when I'm doing something I don't like, it goes slower," he tried to explain.

"I know exactly what you mean," Rose said.

"Like the expression 'time flies when you're having fun?'" Lonn clarified.

"Yeah, like that," Kenai said. "But it's like that expression is really true, and not an expression, it's just that we can't measure time that way, at least not yet."

"Maybe you'll be the one to figure out how to measure it, then?" his dad encouraged. "It sounds like a space-time problem to me."

"As if that kind of time is in another space, one that exists in our minds," Rose added.

Kenai looked hard at Rose. He knew where she was going with that idea, but just wasn't ready to let his dad in on their secrets. She got the message, and turned the conversation in another direction.

"Do you guys always talk like this?" she asked.

"Like what?" Lonn responded.

"About ideas," she said.

"I guess so," Kenai answered. "I never really thought about it that way."

"We never talk that way at my house," she replied.

"What do you talk about?" Lonn asked.

"Money," she blurted out. "I mean," she said, trying to save herself, "we don't talk about much, just normal things."

"Normal things?" Kenai asked.

"Yeah," she said, "mostly about what happened in the day."

"Every family's different," Lonn said.

"How did you and Mrs. Lurie meet?" Rose asked.

"What makes you ask that?" he responded.

"I guess it's just that you seem like such a nice family, I was just wondering," Rose explained.

"We actually met in Italy," Lonn said. "We were both in Rome for our junior year abroad, during college, but we didn't know each other very well. It wasn't until our senior year back at school when we were both taking this agricultural class that we connected.

"Naomi and I were just friends then; I actually had a girlfriend, so after we graduated, we kind of lost touch. I moved to Seattle for graduate school, while she moved to Denver for nursing school. Then she moved to Portland, Oregon for her first job as a nurse. About ten years later, she went on a solo road trip during her summer vacation, and Seattle was her first stop. She had heard through mutual friends that I still lived there, found my information, and called me. We met up for coffee, and have pretty much been together ever since."

"What happened to your girlfriend?" Rose asked.

"Akiko moved out to Seattle with me after college, and we were together for five years, but it just didn't work out. She got very into the music scene, and I just wasn't cool enough for her anymore," Lonn said, laughing to himself. "When I saw Naomi again, it was like she had never changed. She was just the same, very down-to-earth; she really cared about the world, you know, and was even prettier than I had remembered her. We just weren't ready for each other before."

"Did she finish the road trip?" Kenai asked, not remembering, or perhaps never having heard that part of the story.

"Not really," Lonn said. "We took some side trips around

Washington together, and then it was time for her to go back to Portland. The following year she moved to Seattle, and then a couple of years later, we both got jobs in Aspen and moved to the valley. We wanted to raise our family in the mountains."

"Why did you pick Aspen?"

"I guess because we'd both been there as kids, during the wintertime, and couldn't stop thinking about it. It was kind of a dream come true to move out here together."

Rose desperately wanted to hear more, about why they had adopted Kenai and Desta: could they not have children of their own or had they always wanted to adopt? She felt she had been nosy enough, though, and it was about time for the cavern tour to start.

The group circled around the cavern entrance, in front of a large, steel door, waiting for the guide. Kenai and Rose were finishing up their milkshakes, while Lonn sat on a bench reading a thick book. When the tour began, they stood at the very front of the line.

The caves were dark at first, even with the lights on the side, but soon enough their eyes adjusted to the darkness. They had to be careful of the bats flying around, and of bumping into the rough, scratchy sides. The cavernous hallways opened up into a grand space, with stalagmites and stalactites reaching out for them, pools of water glistening below, flowstones like enormous sheets of bacon layered across the walls, soda straw formations dripping, and tall staircases leading them down to the very bottom of the cave, a half-mile away from the entrance.

It was a miraculous site, an underground playground filled with crystals and sedimentary rock; they felt cold and warm at the same time, enveloped by trapped tepid air, echoes ringing in their ears. The guide told them stories of the miners who axe-picked their way through the caves, all the way out to the other side, overlooking the Glenwood Canyons at Exclamation Point.

"Caves are the last frontier on Earth," the tour guide in uniform khakis said. "We have only explored about twenty-percent of the caves in the world. It is the most dangerous and mysterious kind of exploration." She informed the group that the Glenwood Canyon rocks dated back two billion years to the Precambrian era.

During one stretch of hallways, Kenai and Rose stood close to one another. They could feel and hear each other breathing. Being in the middle of the line, they were directed ahead by the front, and pushed forward by the back. At the end of the path, the guide turned off the lights and had them walk in to the balcony space in silence. When she turned on the fluorescent lights, a scene of crystals sparkled before them, a theatre with no sound or movement, and yet more dramatic than anything they had ever seen on the big screen.

The children stayed at the back of the line for the hike up the one hundred twenty-seven stairs. Lonn gave them their space. They both felt the vibrations of other energy around them, but so far, no spirits had appeared. It was then, as time crept slower and they labored up the steps one-by-one, sometimes two-by-two, that Kenai realized that they wouldn't have to dig for any box or journal after all.

When they reached the top of the first landing, Kenai leaned over to Rose and whispered, "Why don't we just have Manu go back in time and find Alma's journals then, and read them to us directly?"

"Well, it seemed to work alright in that movie about going back to the future," she said.

"What movie?" he asked, confused.

"Oh, that's right," she said. "You don't have a TV."

"Well, don't make me feel bad about it," he said.

"No, I didn't mean it like that," she said, apologetically. "It's just that, well, it's just that, I can't imagine my house without a TV, it's the centerpiece of the house. I don't like it, though. I'd rather not have one, but what would my mom do without one? It's her life."

Kenai wanted to get back to his brilliant idea, and didn't have time for self-pity. "We should ask Manu if he could do that," Kenai said. "It may work, who knows? Maybe he even read some of that stuff once, and just didn't tell us about it."

"That's true," she said.

Lonn met up with them, and they continued up the next flight of stairs. They reveled in the compressed expanse, a ballroom of grottos. He put his hand on his son's shoulder. Rose invited him into another conversation.

"Do you ever miss living in a city?" she asked him.

"Sometimes, but we just think raising our children in this valley is an amazing opportunity. What do you think, Kenai? Do you like living here?"

"Yeah, it's beautiful," he answered. "But, I want to live in a big city one day, when I get older," he said.

Lonn patted his son on the back as they continued their upward trek.

It was getting late, but the three of them decided to go on one more adventure. There was a brand new ride, the Cliffhanger Roller Coaster. At 7,100 feet in elevation, it was the highest elevation roller coaster in North America. Zooming up, down and around on Iron Mountain, they could glimpse at the Colorado River 1,450 feet below. It was the perfect ending to a perfect day, their stomachs stuck in their chests, their heads stuck in the billowing clouds, their hearts stuck in a bright half-moon marking the new lavender expanse, refreshed from the overcast day.

As much as Rose tried to hold onto the time, fully conscious of how happy she was as they made their way down the gondola, into the car, and on the road home, listening attentively to the classical music on the public radio station, she knew she was only making time go faster.

When they reached Carbondale with Mount Sopris's glory welcoming them back down to the Crystal Valley, the two stretches of road her family dubbed "Deer Meadow One" and "Deer Meadow Two" revealed Marble's Chair Mountain with its exaggerated swoop and armrest, beckoning them from the hazy distance. She prayed that Lonn would drive on past Redstone, and past Paonia, past Grand Junction, past Salt Lake City, past Nevada, past California, past the Pacific Ocean, Asia, Russia, Europe, anywhere but home. She was so blissful she didn't want the day to end, and yet, soon enough, there they were already, passing the 'Redstone 9" sign, passing Avalanche Creek, passing Filoha Meadows, passing the enormous rock in the river, taking a left onto the back road, past the camp sites, the firehouse, the *Population: 97* wood sign, and then it was done, and she was back in her house, with her mom, just in time to speak to her dad on the phone, who was calling from Atlanta.

"Hi, honey," he said, his voice gravely, distant.

"Hi, Dad," she said, and then started to cry. She hadn't expected to, but all the emotions from the day left her vulnerable.

"It's okay, baby, don't cry. It's going to be alright," he said, hoping to assure her. "I'm sorry, but this is just better for all of us for a while."

"I know," she said, trusting him.

"Sometimes people just need to take a break to understand things better," he said. "And there's work for me to do here, and that's good, too."

"Mom told me. I just wish you would've said goodbye," she said, sniffling. "That's all."

"I wanted to, Rosie," he said. "But I was afraid if I saw you, I wouldn't have left, and I needed to. I'm not a bad person, Rosie," her dad said, seeking reassurance.

"I know, but you shouldn't drink," she said.

"I'm sorry," he said, embarrassed. "Can I talk to your mom?"

"Mom," Rose turned toward her mother. "Dad wants to talk to you."

"Rosie, Rosie." Her dad got louder to make sure she could hear him. "I love you. We'll talk tomorrow, okay? I'm just kind of tired now. Been a long drive, you know."

"I know," she said. "I love you."

"I love you, too, pumpkin. Good night."

Rose pushed the phone at her mom and ran to her bedroom. She was too exhausted to feel anything more. As soon as she threw her backpack onto the floor and put her head on her pillow, she fell sound asleep, and didn't wake up until the next morning, in her clothing, her mouth germy from not brushing her teeth the night before, hungry and thirsty, her brain fuzzy from a million crazy and terrifying dreams of dirty, exhausted, asthmatic miners caked with black coal from head to toe, wandering the Redstone Boulevard, all of them disfigured – broken arms and legs, amputated feet and hands, broken spines and head gashes, missing ears and eyes, skin charred from fire. They were marching in rows, searching for restitution. In one dream, a middle-aged man, hunched over and missing his left arm from the elbow down, stared at Rose, who was floating above him, and begged her with tears streaming down his face: "*Ci libera! Ci libera!*"

13

"*I* suppose it could work," Manu said to the children. "I've never seen the journal before with my own eyes, it was only something I vaguely knew about."

"Well, can you try?" they asked.

So, Manu left the children to venture into space-time, to see if he could read Lady Bountiful's journal to them in real-time. Maybe they could avoid digging for it and getting in trouble, uncovering the answers they needed sooner rather than later.

Manu reconnected one afternoon, as his physical past self was cleaning dishes. He tried to tell himself to go into Mrs. Osgood's room, and search through her drawers, but his physical person could not reconcile the request. It felt like a battle between competing consciousnesses, and the future ghost simply could not win. He could not alter the physical reality of pulling out drawers and flipping pages. Without a body, he just couldn't alter the past, and he could not beat out the domination of his past state of mind.

He returned to the children and no physical time had passed at all. He told them that it was impossible for him to locate a physical object that he had never touched when he was alive. They would have to go ahead and dig up that hole by the river if they wanted to read what Mrs. Osgood had written.

"I know," Rose said. "What if you find a time when Mrs. Osgood was reading and writing in her journal, and then you look over her shoulder and read to us as you are reading yourself?"

"Hmm," he said, "that's not a bad idea. You mean look over her as a spirit from today, not as person from the past?"

"Yes," Rose said.

"You mean, even though my body was alive then, I can go back to that time as a spirit?" Manu asked again.

"Exactly," she said.

"Okay," he said. "It's worth a try."

Soon enough he remembered a dream he had as a person then, about a journal and some letters of Mrs. Osgood's. Perhaps that was the meeting of the future and the present and the past all together? All wrapped up in one single dream? No wonder dreams were so confusing! Manu shared these feelings with the children.

Then in a flash, there he was, standing behind Mrs. Osgood, simply because he had envisioned himself there. She was sitting at her Persian writing desk, in her long, silk nightgown. She was in tears. Mr. Osgood stomped into the room, heavy-footed. As the scene unfolded, Manu recounted the events to the children.

"Damn it, Cleve!" she yelled at him, without turning her head. "You just cannot go and shoot someone, not in our home, not anywhere! Do you understand? Who are you?"

"Lower your voice, woman!" he said in a loud whisper, spitting between his teeth.

"We were not anything more than friends; he was my friend, Cleve, my friend! Can I not have any friends?" she cried, leaving tears on her opened journal. She closed it then.

"Let me see that book!" he said.

"No!" She pulled it to her chest. "This is for me!"

"What is that? Love poems for him?" he said snidely, and went to grab it from her. She quickly shoved it in the drawer and locked it with the brass skeleton key hanging from a long rope around her neck.

"Cleve, no, I told you we were never romantic. You were the one who brought him here from Florence in the first place. You said he was the perfect artist to fix my mirror! You were the one who spent hours talking with him at the Pitti Palace, and you were the one who paid for his expenses to come here, and he did a beautiful job. You know he did. Look at those vines and flowers," she said while sobbing and moving over to the diamond dust mirror over her boudoir. "What do you care anyway? You're never around, and when you are around, all you do is talk about business and money!"

"Well, who else is going to pay for this place? It costs a fortune to run," he yelled, pointing a finger at her.

"Leave," she cried and grabbed his finger to lower it. "Leave me alone, now, or I'll pack up my suitcase and leave this house forever!"

"You wouldn't do that, you wouldn't do that to me, or else!"

he shouted, threateningly.

"Or else, what?" she defied him. "You know I don't care about all these, these, these things," she said, gesturing a full circle with her arms outstretched. "I never have. It's not why I fell in love with you, why I married you, why I moved here. You know that, Cleve. Now leave me!"

Mr. Osgood opened his mouth to argue, but turned on his heels instead and left, slamming the door behind him.

She fell on the floor, sobbing until her face was completely blotched red. When she could catch her breath again, she unlocked her drawer, and pulled out the leather-bound journal. She opened it to its middle, and began writing furiously. Manu knelt down beside her, hoping his presence could somehow comfort her. He read out loud to the children as she wrote. Her handwriting was clear, yet feminine and delicate:

> *Oh my dear Arthur. I'm so sorry I left you like I did. How could I know what the future would hold? How could I know that I would be left with such a cruel and ruthless man? You were so gentle, so kind to me, and I ran as far as I could from you. No wonder you lost your mind. You saw what I only now see. Where are you now? Are you resting peacefully? I miss our talks, our rides together, just sitting near you. I miss you, my dear friend and am sorry for all the pain I inflicted. I'm sorry, so sorry...*
>
> *I would have forgotten about you, almost completely, were it not for those dreams. Several years after your death, I came upon a*

book that reminded me of you. It was a George Eliot book, of course, and as soon as I saw it, listened to its poetic and intelligent words again, I dreamed of you. It was a passionate dream; we found each other and loved each other as if we existed in eternity, wrapped up in each other's arms.

But not all the dreams were like that, in fact hardly any other ones were like that. That was the most connected I had ever felt to you in a dream, actually, but there were so many other ways that you appeared in my dreams. One time, your name was printed in blocks of rainbow colors; in another you were my pen, a pen I was using to write a letter with, to whom I can't remember now. In one, we held each other as swarms of people passed us by. Other times you showed me your life, your wife and sons, but when I asked your children's names, you refused to answer. Another time I was waiting for you in a house surrounded by people I didn't recognize. I knew you'd be coming around the corner, completely unsuspecting of me, and when you entered the house and saw me sitting on the couch, you were happy. Then you told me you weren't happy at all in your world, but we were happy sitting together; Cleve sat at my left, upset but fully aware that he could do nothing about our strong connection.

At times in the dreams, you didn't want me

near, you were almost repulsed by me, but other times, you wanted me close, and I would wake with the most pure feelings of love I have ever experienced. I must have had fifty or sixty dreams of you over a period of three years, and they still come to me now and again. And so I ask over and over, why? Why you? Are you a symbol of something I longed for, or a representation of your true self, or of me, with you as my mirror?

She stopped writing suddenly, letting the pen fall from her hand. She curled herself up in a ball, and rocked back and forth, clutching the journal to her chest.

"I am reaching for her, wrapping her in my arms, even though I know she can't really feel me. She is looking all around the room, as if she's feeling me, but not understanding how," Manu said to the children.

Her crying subsided soon afterwards, and she stood up, facing the fireplace. She threw the small book into the smoldering fire that warmed her room, as if it were a sport, and she watched every last piece of it burn, until only the leather cover remained, buried under the ashes and iron log holder.

"Then what was she burying by the river?" Rose asked Manu immediately.

"I have no idea," Manu said, his voice low, as if traveling from another place.

"You didn't know you could do that?" Kenai asked. "You've never gone back in time before like that, to a new situation? Have you?"

Manu was quiet with disbelief. He was still in the bedroom with Lady Bountiful, and yet he was also by the river with the children. He was in both places at one time, relating the past to the present. And all it took was the will for him to do it. It was so easy, and yet impossible beforehand without the idea of its possibility.

He had never read her journal when he knew her, never truly understood her complexity and torment until now.

"What happened next?" the children asked with unbounded enthusiasm, their eyes aglow with the magic of storytelling.

Manu told them that he felt a responsibility, a deep responsibility to have them all move on from the hundred year-old drama. He also understood from the children's description of Mr. Osgood pacing back and forth in the game room that Mr. Osgood, and his indentured staff, needed closure as well. They were all keeping Redstone locked within their sadness, when Redstone was no longer theirs to have.

Returning to the space-time from over a hundred years ago, Manu described watching his physical self awake from the dream, drenched in sweat and disoriented. His physical self knew it had just experienced an intense dream; he remembered Mr. and Mrs. Osgood were in it, and there were also some children he could not identify, but somehow he seemed to know them well. There were also a lot of words, many stories within the story. The dream was so vivid, so real to him, that he swore he would never forget it.

Manu looked as if it was all too much for him to synthesize. "I am a spirit," he thought out loud to the children. "So how is it that I can still feel, and be hurt by something new? How is it that I feel more alive now than I ever did back then?"

He was starting to become weary. He explained to the children that he wanted to come to peace with his life in Redstone, with Lady Bountiful. He wanted to move on, he wanted to be set free, and to free himself from the children. They said that they needed to move on, too, as much as they were captivated by the story, they needed to return to their own stories.

"Lady Bountiful seems to have made it to the beyond, so why can't I?" Manu asked the children.

Perhaps it was in the dream world where all his selves could meet, Rose thought, where time criss-crossed, and different lifetimes coalesced. It was a confusing, messy place, this dream world, an intersection of infinite portals, a place of eternal possibilities.

"How do we know that she's passed on?" Rose asked.

And there it was, the great looming unknown: *Had* Lady Bountiful passed on, or was she still haunting the town, too? Manu had never seen her, never heard her, never felt her; Rose and Kenai hadn't either, but that didn't mean anything. They needed to find out now, however; they needed to locate her spirit and find out if it was still around, to know for sure where she was.

14

*I*t was Labor Day weekend, and the town of Redstone was celebrating its annual art fair. The streets were lined with cars and people; a white tent on the Inn's lawn covered the artists and their work. School had officially started the week before, but everyone knew that school didn't really begin until after Labor Day weekend.

Rose invited Kenai to come over to her house to play while her mom ran some errands in town. Just that morning her mom had retreated to her usual self-pity rant. She was mostly talking out loud, but she also wanted Rose to hear: "I just don't know how my life turned out like this. Promise me, Rosie, that you won't make the same mistakes I did. I had so much potential, and I just threw it all away. Don't waste your life, Rosie. Don't be me, please. Find something you like to do, that you're good at, and stick with it, okay? Don't ever stop working. Don't marry someone so, so, so different from you, don't do it, Rosie. Do you hear me?"

"Yes, Mom, I hear you. I won't, okay? I won't waste my life," Rose said in a flat voice.

Her mom threw a fit until she went outside for a smoke. It was the same old story. Her mom would make some progress, pay a little attention to her for awhile, and then it was back to feeling sorry for herself. Her mom left soon after that to go grocery shopping and get her nails done.

Rose and Kenai decided to invite Manu from inside Rose's home. As this was a new place for them to contact Manu, Rose sang a new song for him. It was a song about the sun and tomorrow, another one of her all-time-favorites. Manu showed up after the end of the second chorus, sitting on her bed.

"Well, this is strange," Manu said. He pointed to the left corner. "That's where I used to sleep. And my sisters slept here," he said, patting his hand on her bed. "So, children, I have to tell you that I am getting pretty tired of this game, but it has made me realize that it's time to pass onto the other side. I know what's going on here, for all us spirits. We are all waiting for Lady Bountiful to return, so we can move on, because that's what Mr. Osgood is waiting for, and it's his force that's got us all stuck. I propose that we find a way to get her back, to communicate with her somehow."

"A séance!" Rose exclaimed.

"A what?" Manu asked.

"You don't know what a séance is? It's when we call for spirits, and supposedly it works, if you have the right medium," she explained.

"Well, then, who would that be?" Kenai asked. "I don't know any mediums, do you?"

"You both found me, why couldn't you find Mrs. Osgood?" Manu asked the children.

They both thought about it for a minute.

"Fine," Kenai said. "We'll take on the challenge, but we have to figure out a lot of things beforehand. Like, where do we find a medium without other people knowing what we're up to? And, where should we do it?"

"At the castle, of course," Rose answered.

"Right," Kenai said.

They discussed many of the details: the where, when, and how. With Patricia on their side, they could get inside one night, but which night? A full moon? A new moon?

Deeply involved in their planning, they heard a knocking at the front door. The children went to the door, and Manu followed along. It was Kenai's family.

"Kee," Naomi said. "It's hot; we all want to go swimming. We're going to the Snowmass pool. Rose, do you want to join us?"

"I don't know if I can; let me call my mom and find out," Rose answered.

"Okay, well, we're getting our things together now, so let us know soon," she requested. "We'd love to have you join us."

"Ten more minutes, Kenai," Lonn said, holding Desta in his arms.

"Kee, Kee," Desta said, pushing her way out of her father's arms to join her brother.

"I'll be home soon, Dee Dee," Kenai said to his sister in a quiet voice, touching her chubby arm.

Lonn pulled Desta nearer to him, and closed the door behind them.

"Those are your parents, Kenai?" he asked in a most peculiar manner.

"Yeah," Kenai replied. "I'm adopted, so's my sister."

"I can see that, no, that's not what I meant. Those are my parents, too!" he said, beaming.

"What do you mean?" Kenai asked.

"I mean, those are my parents, were my parents, their spirits, I can feel their spirits even though they look different, they feel exactly the same. They've come back for me. They're looking for me!" he said with incredible delight. He was dancing around the room. "They know I am stuck here! But they've found me now. They found me! I know I have to go home now! I knew it; it's time to go home!"

"And is Desta your sister too?" Kenai asked, curious and confused all at the same time.

"Oh no," he said. "I don't know who she is, but those are my parents, I am sure of it!" Manu continued to dance around the room, spinning in circles, and jumping for joy.

"Well, then," Rose said as an announcement. "There's no doubt now that we have to help you pass over, and that we are absolutely the ones to help you."

"That doesn't mean my parents have to die now, does it?" Kenai asked with fear building up in his throat. He had never felt such love for his parents, or such a connection.

"No, no, not at all," Manu said. "I told you, time means nothing once you have passed over. As soon as I get there, they will be there, too, no matter how long they've lived on Earth."

"That doesn't make any sense," Kenai said. "Time exists here, but not over there? How can our spirits be in so many places at once, while our bodies can only be in one place at a time?" Kenai asked.

"I know, it's complicated, and hard to understand, *mio caro ragazzo*," Manu explained as best he could. "This is what I know to be true: the role of time in the universe is to account for change. Time exists because of change. So, when things are changing, we have time to observe it. Now, there is a part of the universe where nothing changes at all, ever. It is as it was in the beginning. When we are in that place, time does not exist, because nothing changes there. A physical body, however, is the definition of change. Our bodies are always changing, and so when we inhabit our bodies, we are changing, and therefore living in a world of time. Does that make sense?"

"Is that why our bodies can't go to that place, the place where nothing changes, where there isn't time?" Rose interrupted.

"Yes," Manu said, answering Rose's question. "Let's call that place the non-physical world. It is a place of pure energy, no mass, where the laws of our physical universe don't apply. And so our spirits can be anywhere at anytime, too, because our spirits don't have any mass, or weight; our spirits are not physical. But what I am learning now, through this experience, is how our spirits can exist in the physical world, even though they are not physical. I have seen that we can't change the past, no matter what. We can spiritually return to the past, but we can't physically. I tried that, and it simply doesn't work, except in the dream world, which I suppose, must be a parallel universe."

"So, wait," Rose said, trying to understand. "Is that why they call it physics? Because that part of science just explains physical things, not non-physical things?"

"Well, I never thought of it that way, *dolcezza*," Manu said affectionately. He was feeling a lot of love around the children now. The space among them was changing, the vibrations slowing down.

"I suppose so," he continued. "I only learned a little bit of physics when I was alive. Mrs. Osgood was more fond of literature, history and philosophy. She taught me almost as much as she knew about those subjects. She would pass any book, magazine or newspaper she read onto me, and then we would talk about it. She filled my head with so many ideas, it drove my papa *pazzo*, really crazy, but there was nothing he could do about it. She was Lady Bountiful, and everyone loved her. She dressed the whole town in the best of fashions, she filled our school with hundreds of books, she turned holidays into magical events. But she did fill my head so much, that when she went away, I couldn't stop thinking about her, about ideas, about love, my mind was always in the clouds, I couldn't pay attention to anything, and in the end, that's what caused my death."

The children realized then that they had never asked Manu about how he had died. But now that he had mentioned it, it seemed as good a time as ever to ask him about it.

"How did you die?" Rose asked boldly, no longer afraid of scaring, and ultimately, losing Manu.

"It was silly, really, very silly," he said. He described how he was hiking near Marble, near the Crystal City Mill where they mined silver, lead, copper, iron and zinc. Manu had gone by himself, because he always did his best thinking alone. Once Mrs. Osgood left town for good, he had no one else with whom he could really converse. Most people started to think of him as crazy, like his father, but worse. He couldn't concentrate on anything but love. He missed Mrs. Osgood terribly, even though he knew she could never love him in that way. He dreamed of finding someone like her, someone he could marry, someone he could have a family with, but he also couldn't imagine who that person could be if it wasn't her. Who would he find in his tiny, abandoned town to replace her, he thought. He realized then that he had to leave; he would have to go somewhere else to fall in love, a big city, most likely. Perhaps to France, to Paris, where he had heard Mrs. Osgood was living, but that was no way to get over her, he believed.

He was thinking so hard, he said, that he got too close to a cliff; there were too many loose rocks near the ledge. Maybe there had been a rockslide recently, he had guessed; it was springtime and the rains came down heavy. And he fell, just like that, he fell, down, down, down the crevice, even though to this day he still didn't remember getting to the bottom. All he remembered was rolling, then rushing down the mountain with rocks, dirt, roots, mud, scraping his body, his hands. He tried desperately to hold on, but couldn't get a grip anywhere, and then his body rolled over an even steeper cliff, so that he was in midair, and that was it, that's all he remembered seeing, or feeling, until he felt lifted through space, like through a door in the middle of the air, where there was no pain, no fear; but soon enough, it felt like an enclosure, and the only movement he could control returned him back through the same door he came through; he couldn't find the door on the other end of the middle space, though. And ever since then, all he could do was go back and forth through that same opening, into a kind of middle world.

There was another knocking at Rose's door. More than ten minutes had passed since Kenai's dad and Desta had left Rose's house. Rose quickly grabbed a bathing suit, towel and sweat-shirt, and wrote a note for her mother telling her where she would be. She didn't call her mom to ask for permission because she didn't want to take the chance that her mother would say no.

"We have to go," Kenai said in Manu's direction, but Manu had already disappeared.

The children ran to the front door where Lonn was waiting for them.

"Your mother's been waiting," Lonn said, somewhat annoyed, the first time Rose had ever heard that tone in his otherwise kind voice.

"I know. I'm sorry," Kenai said, hanging his head.

"What were you doing?" Lonn asked.

"Nothing really," Kenai said.

"Nothing, really?" Lonn repeated.

"We were finishing up a puzzle we were working on and lost track of time," Rose said.

"Okay," Lonn said, unconvinced, but leaving the discussion alone. "Kenai, get your stuff together, quickly. And apologize to your mother for keeping her."

"I will, I will," Kenai yelled back at his father as he ran into the house. Rose and Lonn were standing together near the car. She had an urge to tell Lonn everything, everything about the spirits, everything about everything, but she left it alone, too. She tried to imagine Lonn as Manu's father, but she couldn't; it was too hard for her to see.

And then Lonn said to Rose, completely unprompted, "Do you like Italian food?"

She was taken aback and didn't respond. Italian food. Why was Kenai's dad, Manu's dad – Manu's Italian dad - all of a sudden talking about Italian food?

"Italian food, do you like it, Rose?" he asked again.

"Oh, of course, why?" she asked as nonchalantly as she possibly could, pretending she hadn't heard him the first time.

"Because there's a new Italian restaurant I wanted to try, and was thinking maybe we'd all stop there on the way home. Think you can stay with us that long?"

"Sure, I'm sure it would be fine," Rose replied.

She knew, absolutely knew, at that very moment, that there was no such thing as a coincidence. And then she wondered how many thoughts did she have during the day that came from somewhere completely different than from where she thought they had come. We control our own thoughts, don't we? she wondered. Don't we? she asked herself again, and again, and for the rest of the day, at Snowmass, as they swam in the heated pool, played in the park, and ate Italian food in Basalt, the small town between Snowmass and Carbondale.

She was aware that she was somewhere else in her mind for almost the whole day, but she couldn't shake it. She was somewhere else, and then a few scattered rain showers delivered a pair of rainbows, the first one as clear as a white chalk line on a blackboard, the second arc a reflection of the first, and she wished she could fly over them in a hot air balloon, and never, ever return home.

She envisioned herself soaring high above the valley, looking down on the Elk Mountain Range's Maroon Bells, two ragged bell-shaped peaks often white-lined across from snow, both reaching over 14,000 feet; the Bells continued to be the most photographed spot in all of Colorado. Her parents were married at the welcome center there during a late summer three years before she was born; on one of their wedding anniversaries, she hiked with them about a mile up to Maroon Lake, a basin carved out by glaciers during the Ice Age and subsequently dammed by rockslides. An earthmoving company working at a reservoir site in the Snowmass area had recently discovered bones from an Ice Age mammoth, which were then excavated by paleontologists, nicknamed the "Snowmastadon," and put on display at the Denver Museum of Nature and Science.

With her mind now in the clouds, Rose let her imagination hop off the hot air balloon and catch a breathtaking ride with the gargantuan Snowmastadon all the way down the rocky Bells, where she landed back safely to her real life with Kenai as her very best friend in the whole, entire cosmos.

Part 2: Lady Bountiful

15

I walk the hallways, over and over again, not exactly sure
what it is I am hoping to find. For the most part, I have
stayed away from the castle; it isn't my home anymore, hasn't
been my home since 1911 when we shuttered the windows and
mothballed the furniture.

Nobody seems to notice my presence at the Inn, however,
and that's just fine for me. I'm trying to protect myself from all the
other spirits who have trouble keeping to themselves. I try to
explain to them that we are all stuck here, will be for awhile until
Cleve releases the spell, and so they might as well enjoy the
space, in peace, until then.

George, a former bartender, has a grand time making a nui-
sance of himself. He finds pleasure in scaring the poor innocents

and will take no direction from me. Recently he meddled in a young newly engaged couple's business, and the next morning the young woman was left alone and her fiancé, well, let's just say he was found lying flat, dead, on the pavement right below his window. I can't say exactly what happened, I don't think anyone knows for sure, but it's extremely disturbing, and I have a feeling George had something to do with it. His laughter is so alive, it penetrates the natural barrier, and many of the guests can hear it ripple through the walls.

This afternoon I hear children talking, and then I hear Manuele's voice. I've never felt him here. Others tell me he stays closer to the river, and I don't want to disturb his space. I'm part of the reason he's stuck here, too. I know that, and it makes me feel sad and guilty. But today his voice is clear and joyous, and emanating from Room 208, the room with the broken lock that no one ever bothers to fix.

I rest outside the door and overhear them all talking about me.

"When guests arrived," Manuele explains to the children, "Mrs. Osgood would stand by the small window in her bedroom that we called the 'peering window' to see what the women were wearing. She always wanted to be in the same fashion as her guests, *bellissima* to make them feel comfortable. Some thought that she was so insecure she needed to copy them, but those people didn't know her. They were just jealous, and never lasted long working at the castle."

Hearing his voice brings back so many memories, so many feelings from that time, I find my spirit slipping through the door, almost being pulled through it, practically against my will, and then, suddenly, it's too late. He feels me, and so do the children.

I appear in my white lace high-necked dress; it's how they

want to see me, a copy of the photo framed on the stairs of the Inn. They recognize me at once.

I disappear within myself, but then, wanting to be known, reappear.

No one says a word. They stare hard, until faint smiles curve around their lips.

"What?" I ask. "You look like you've just seen a ghost."

Their laughter breaks the silence.

"I told you she was funny," Manuele says. "Most people didn't know that about her, how funny she was."

"You can refer to me directly, Manuele. I am here now," I say.

I can tell that he just doesn't know what to do with the information, with my presence. The young girl speaks up.

"It's just that we met here today to figure out a way to call you back. We were trying to figure out how to do a séance, how we would break into the castle, or be let into the castle, or how-" Rose begins to explain.

"I don't go to the castle," I say.

"You don't?" Manuele asks.

"I have stayed away from the castle. I can feel that Cleve wants me to return, but I'm not ready and have no idea when I will ever be. He wants me so terribly, I am afraid of being held there forever."

"But why are you stuck here?" the girl inquires.

"It's Mr. Osgood. He has an enormous energy field that he still doesn't know how to use properly. He was out of control while in his body, and he's out of control in this Middle World, too."

"But how did you escape him when you were alive?" Rose asks.

"That is an excellent question, my dear. And if I tell you that,

I will have to start at the very beginning," I say. "Would you like me to tell you the story of Alma?"

"The story of Alma?" Rose asks for clarification.

"Yes, because I am not just Alma anymore, but a combination of every person I was and ever will be," I say.

"Yes, of course we want to hear the story of Alma!" she says, not too interested at this point in learning about my other lives.

"Can we meet somewhere else less, less...contained?" I ask.

We all transfer to the river. I follow them there, and we rest among the rocks. It feels good to be in the open space with other souls, free from man-made enclosures. In the clear.

16

I introduce the story from its beginning, or from where I deem the beginning to be. I recall the dialogue from our first encounter as if it were yesterday, because in my mind it nearly is.

"Dance with me," he said the first time we met.

"Pardon," I said. I wanted to hear his accent again.

"Dance with me," he repeated.

An American, I thought to myself. He had a broad face with whiskers that curled up around his cheeks. He was on the shorter side and a tad portly. He stood erect.

I let him take my hands.

He led me around the dance floor. He knew of the customary waltz. He had danced here before. He looked carefully into my eyes – not too long, not too quickly, as one watches a carriage pass by, curious of its passengers, yet cautious of one's manners.

After two dances he asked to sit with me.

"What brings you here?" I asked.

"I'm looking for money," he said.

"You Americans are bold, aren't you?"

"You asked," he said.

I moved my chair slightly away from his.

"You Europeans are quite good at wasting time," he said.

"I'm Swedish," I said.

"Sweden isn't part of Europe?" he joked.

"Scandinavia," I answered seriously.

"I see," he said, teasing me. "Do I frighten you?" he asked.

"I don't think so," I replied.

"You don't think so?"

"I'm not sure," I answered, smiling.

"But you must have a feeling?" he asked.

"Many," I said.

"Generally or presently?"

"Both," I said.

I saw my sister looking at us from across the room.

"Are you here alone?" I asked.

"Yes. And you?" he asked.

"I am here with my family."

"You must be royalty, then."

"Why do you say that?" I asked.

"Only royal families travel in packs," he said.

"Is that true?" I asked.

"You tell me."

I paused then said, "Yes, from my experience, I would have to say that's true."

I returned my chair to its original position.

"And your title?" he asked.

"They call me a countess," I replied.

"What does a countess do exactly?" he asked.

"Look for American tycoons at foreign receptions," I replied.

"I wouldn't say that I'm a tycoon. Not yet, at least," he said.

I stood up, and then he did.

He looked around the imposing Grand Hall.

"So immense," he said. "The gold is blinding."

I looked to the ceiling. The chandeliers hung like giant sea anemones.

"Cardon has always been one of my favorites," I said, referring to the four murals entitled: *Dawn, Morning, Day,* and *Dusk.* "I like the darkness somehow."

"He's not an original, you know," he said.

"That's alright," I said. "He can still be a fine artist."

"I prefer more intimate settings."

"I don't think kings have a choice in how they live."

There was silence.

And then some more silence.

My sister had made her way to the corner of the room, arm-in-arm with her suitable husband, but her eyes were still focused on me. We both looked her way together, and she turned away.

"I must be going," I said.

"Like I guessed – in packs," he said.

"There is always one who strays from the pack, sir."

"I see, madam."

"Miss," I said, correcting him.

"You know English better than I do," he said.

I smiled.

"When can I see you again?" he asked.

"I don't know," I said. "But I'm sure you'll find a way, eventually." I began to walk away when he called to me.

"Don't you want to know my name?" he asked.

"I suppose so," I said.

"John Cleveland Osgood," he said, and then waited a moment. "But you can call me Cleve."

"Cleve," I said, to know how it felt to say his name aloud.

"And you are?" he asked.

"Alma Regina Shelgrem."

"Alma," he said. "Soul."

"Yes, soul."

I turned away from him then. I couldn't go on with this anymore, not in public. I looked for my sister, and refused to look behind me. When I caught up with her at the entrance, she stared at me with the expected disapproval. She had a pretty yet masculine face – blond hair, more fair than mine, midday blue-sky eyes, sharp edges, shallow cheeks. Although younger than I by a few years, she still acted as my mother. She had done as she was supposed to: married correctly, followed traditions, even if I was born to set the example, she filled that open space as soon as it was apparent I wouldn't. Instead of being proud of her conquest, confident in her coveted position, she resented my freedom, the freedom that, I often reminded her, had been created for me.

We were spending our last night at the Belgium Palace in Brussels, the home of King Leopold II. Walking up the Grand Staircase, lines surrounded us. Large blocks of marble at every turn, new and bright, like tombs waiting for their dead. There was a harmonious geometry in the space, but still I felt insignificant. Maybe grandeur is a way of feeling small, I thought, of keeping one sane. Smallness, while intimate, may bring along too much intimacy, and chaos. No place to hide. I should have remembered this years later.

My sister began to speak once we reached the top of the staircase as we sauntered to the bedrooms. I didn't want to talk about my male conversationalist. I didn't want her to live vicariously through me. I wanted to keep this one all to myself. This one was different. He wanted to play my game; he even seemed to enjoy it.

There is nothing worse than being bored of life, and I did everything I could to fight this boredom. I created romantic angst when there was none, pining over boys who I knew could never bring me happiness, but who provided me with something to do, something to think about, something to obsess over, just to feel some semblance of passion. A few of those boys bit, more didn't. Of course those who didn't bite were more amusing and painful, as I wallowed in comforting self-pity for the unrequited love I so deserved.

I read novels, trying to identify with any of the characters, but I never felt truly connected to any of them. They were always outside of me, and I, the ignorant, pathetic observer. Even in my previously arranged marriage, I still yearned for something else. When my first husband died suddenly, only a year into our union, I felt such a surge of guilt, I ran away to America, to New York, only to return to Sweden, running away again, this time from an obsessive courter, a Mr. Arthur Cobb, who turned out not to be who he said he was.

My family and I started our long journey back to Sweden from Belgium the next morning after meeting Cleve at the palace. My sister and her husband commented on the verdant scenery and teased each other about facts and figures. Mother and Father also rode in our train car and bothered one another throughout the ride – he went on and on about politics, and she complained of the distant company and gaudy room they stayed in at the palace. He made her chuckle, at times.

I was quiet for most of the endless and blissful ride through Belgium and into Germany, dreaming of Cleve, of escaping to America once again, running into the mystery of it all, of growing up, finally, of being who I always thought I was. Royalty meant nothing anymore. Not all is *ordning och reda*. Though I knew nothing of this man, nothing at all about him, he seemed so commanding and mysterious and playful. I acted the disinterested part as all ladies are instructed to do, but inside fell in love with him after our first dance together that fateful night.

My family and I stopped for a week in Berlin to rest. As they all went sightseeing, I escaped to cafes and bookshops. My German was adequate, although not fluent by any measure. I comprehended far better than I could speak. The youth debated with one another in profound fervor, in such dramatic urgency to state their opinions before the other, as if life itself depended on each retort, making me feel more at home somehow than actually being at home.

It was a challenge to understand every sentence, but I could make out enough meaning if the table held the same company for at least fifteen minutes. They condemned America for its blatant capitalism and individualism, and yet I intuited some envy behind their criticisms. Walking the hard surfaces in Berlin, the gritty alleys, overcast mornings, people avoiding people, block after block, as both buoys and ships in a regatta, feeling the hard city pulse beneath me, the city's horse carriages depositing sewage and stench, the artists and philosophers huddling in corners with their tall mugs of beer, cheering, clinking with one another, sometimes throwing things at one another, the debating, and the reveling in intellectual confrontations, it was almost not serious at all because of the seriousness they assigned it when they were safe in their little cafes, and not at war; they were like children, hoping for all citizens of the world to enjoy equality, believing fiercely and tirelessly that people did not work for their advancement in society, that they did not work towards change or by pulling their own selves out of the tar pit, that forgiveness and determination had nothing at all to do with it, that everyone deserved the same things out of life.

I took these ideas and held them so strongly that it was if they were sewn onto my under garments or tattooed onto the small of my back or growing like a baby inside me.

My mother, of course, complained about the dirty city, and the uncouth people, the women especially. The language was much too harsh for her, and the food atrocious. My father found refuge in the voluminous libraries, researching history (the Founding Fathers of America were oddly the greatest source of interest for him) and pouring through the stacks of periodicals. My sister and brother-in-law relished in the architectural tours and design studios. They spotted Impressionist art in the avant-garde galleries and acquired two pieces, one for their bedroom and the other for their sitting room. Both Monet, which he painted while in in Norway.

"Monet?" the girl interrupts my storytelling. "I love Monet! He's one of my favorite artists!"

"You know about Monet?" I ask.

"I like to paint," she says.

Well, I loved those images, too, although I believe my sister and her husband only purchased them because someone else had told them they were beautiful and becoming popular. My sister later shared with me that she heard it was Scandinavia's summer's beauty, really, that struck Monet most because, for some reason, he had not expected it.

Berlin lost some of its appeal for my family by the end of the week, and they were ready to leave.

The subsequent travels home were quick. Once we resettled in Stockholm, nothing much else interested me, except for Cleve. I dreamed only of him, and of America. I prayed every day, riding my horses, playing the piano, humming a children's tune, lying in the grass, hiding in the library huddled around any book I could find in English, eating, not eating, reading in my bedroom, strolling in the gardens, staring at the fountains, bathing, all the while everywhere, constantly, praying.

And then, finally, a letter arrived. From Cleve. He had not forgotten about me!

> **Dear Countess Shelgrem,**
>
> **It was a delight meeting you. Since then, I have not been able to stop thinking of you. This has caused me some distress, however, since I am a married man. I tell you this so that you know I am an honest man, with you. I will not write more about this matter, as I am leaving any possible further communication between us in your hands.**
>
> **Yours affectionately,**
> **Cleve**

And then began the many, many letters that passed between us.

Suddenly a conversation from another space pulls me in, and I pause from recounting my story to the children. Some strangely dressed people are inspecting the Inn. The General Manager is showing them around, relating her version of the building's history. A middle-aged man leading the group asks the majority of the questions. He notices the impending portrait of me on the stair landing. He asks about me.

"That is Mrs. Alma Osgood, John Osgood's second wife. She was called Lady Bountiful by the town," the General Manager responds.

"She's quite beautiful," the man with the half-beard responds. "Very regal, actually."

"Oh, I'm sure she was something, Chris," the manager says. "You should make a film about *her*!"

"Maybe next time," he says, pausing for a moment and then continuing up the carpeted stairs to the landing. "The film we're about to shoot has got me so busy I can't see anything past my nose!"

I don't mind being transported elsewhere like this anymore, even when I am in the center of something else. It used to bother me greatly, the loss of direction over my own whereabouts. But I have learned not to hold onto anything in my current spirit-state, because I have no control of where and who will beckon me.

My spirit seems to respond immediately when it's authentically requested. I have come to welcome these unexpected callings. They keep me alive on Earth. For as long as I am remembered on Earth is how I still exist on Earth, for better or for worse.

"Mrs. Osgood? Mrs. Osgood?" the children desperately call to me.

"My apologies," I reply, reengaging with them and bidding the film director and his crew *adieu.* "I've been a little distracted this afternoon," I say to the boy and girl.

I remember where I had left them in my story and forge ahead.

Cleve hadn't left Europe since meeting me, but had finalized his divorce in the meantime, and we met up in Paris before crossing the Atlantic together. During our travels I told him about Arthur Cobb, a man I met while living in New York who had become obsessed with me.

Arthur said he was the son of an English nobleman who originally came to America to earn his fortune in business. Arthur said he had been a member of the British Royal Guards. First landing in Boston, he soon moved to New York to increase his chances at making money, but he was abysmal at business and henceforth decided to make a living from his passion: horses.

"Is that how you two met? Riding horses?" the girl asks, interrupting me.

"Very perceptive of you, yes, that's how we met. He was my riding teacher. But I don't want to get into the whole story of Arthur, because, well, it's of no consequence now. But I will say, however, that, well, that I was very wrong about him. At the time of our meeting, he was the most interesting man I had ever met, and we seemed to have a lot in common," I explain, conjuring up images of Arthur. A pang of regret and loss grip me, until I release the solemn energy into the ether, and return to memories of Cleve.

Eventually, Cleve asked me to join him in America, and so I took my leap of faith and headed back to America with him. Once we arrived in Redstone, we moved into a ranch house on our property, and immediately started designing and building the castle. We definitely had grand ideas for the castle, as it needed to house some very important people, but I wanted to make sure that it was of a style, on the exterior, that we could build the rest of the town in, so we used the local stone. Inside, however, we decorated using varied influences: an English living room, a Persian library, a Russian dining room, and a French parlor room. There was a hand-pulled elevator to take us up and down the three floors.

Cleve and I got along relatively well throughout the construction because at the time we thought we were working towards one vision, a utopia for all the miners and their families to live far better than any miners ever had. It was supposed to be a model for the rest of the industrial world. Cleve even hired a sociologist to develop the human affairs for our vision. The scientist was Dr. Richard Corwin of Pueblo, Colorado, and he was hired in 1901 to head the Sociological Department of Cleve's company, Colorado Fuel and Iron, or CF&I, as it was often called.

Richard was a fine man; I quite enjoyed his company. I believed he had the best of intentions, as I did. Although I have to say, looking back, I was much more naïve than he was. We cared for many of the same things, but his age had made him cynical. I was still in my early twenties and didn't know then how many sides one person can have to his personality. I didn't know then that selves can get divided, and yet still co-exist.

We further developed the town of Redstone and the coalmine, which we called Coal Basin, at the same time that we were building the castle.

In Redstone, we built a 200-seat amphitheater; a library with hundreds of books; a clubhouse for dances, lantern shows, concerts, and lectures; a billiard room; a card room; and a reading room that the women also used for tea socials and card parties; a general store; a post office; and a doctor's office. We built European-style houses for the families employed in town, each with three to five rooms, painted in matching pastel colors, with plumbing and access to our own electrical grid. For the bachelors and for the miners living in Coal Basin who came to Redstone once a week, we built a dormitory, which you both know as the Redstone Inn.

These were the best years Redstone has ever seen. It was magical, and I was very proud of our accomplishments.

The school we created was top notch. I helped Mrs. Wright and Mrs. Freeman with developing the curriculum. Manuele's sister Adelina was one of our best students.

"She was so smart, *Signora*, wasn't she?" Manuele asks, smiling proudly.

"Very," I say. "And so were you, Manuele. Your parents were very special people. In a way, I always envied them," I say.

"You did?" Manuele asks, astonished.

"Of course," I answer. "To me, they had it all. A beautiful, intelligent family. A great love and respect for one another. A modest and clean home, a safe and beautiful place to live, good and steady work. A peaceful life. What more is there to want from a life on Earth, really?"

Manuele's face lightens at first then soon enough the sides of his mouth turn downwards. I hurry on with the rest of my story.

I was very busy with tending to the town and our families that I paid little attention to Cleve's business. I assumed he was taking care of everything, that he cared for all of us, and was working hard to ensure our good lives there. He was always meeting with this one and that, traveling to New York, Chicago and Europe when necessary. Sometimes I joined him on those trips, where I was able to go to the theatre and do some shopping for our home. Cleve's business partners John Jerome, Alfred Cass and Julian Kebler came around quite often, and we had a grand time together. Late into the evenings I could hear the men argue, but I assumed that was the way of business in America. When the conversations became too loud, they retreated to the game room below, smoking cigars, playing cards or billiards.

Cleve and I had different bedrooms, so I usually never knew how late into the evenings the debating went on. But by morning time, all was usually well, and we would breakfast on the patio overlooking Deer Park, and ride our horses all year long. We listened to concerts in our pagoda by the river during the summers, and played music in the drawing room during the winters. We entertained powerful men and women during this fantastical time. We even secretly entertained King Leopold II of Belgium once, the man who had made our first meeting possible.

It wasn't until a couple of years later, however, that I started to realize how sour Cleve's business was going. There was a hint of trouble about a year after I arrived, but at that time I let myself believe that Cleve had taken care of everything. By then, Cleve limited my knowledge of the business by sharing little with me. I could offer no advice or input. He kept me so much at bay, he told me, so that I could enjoy my life in Redstone. Why worry my pretty little head with such nonsense? he would say. I'm taking care of everything, he assured me. Why should both of us be worried all the time and not take advantage of this paradise we've created? I accepted the compliment and loving care with relish, even if once and awhile I reminded him of my intelligence and my capability, which I was actually beginning to doubt day-by-day, playing the role of the fine, obedient wife.

On one occasion when Cleve, Julian Kebler and I returned to Redstone from a particularly successful business (and shopping!) trip just before the Christmas of 1902 to share our good news of securing the company's finances, we were welcomed with an earthquake. It was actually very exciting, and we interpreted the negligible shake as a good sign of things to come.

Soon enough, however, things went downhill. Quickly. Cleve was forever talking about money, constantly, and how there wasn't enough of it, and if I hadn't spent so much on the house and the village and on lavishing the families with expensive Christmas gifts, he would be in a much better financial position, but now he had to go talk to the "fools in New York," and ask them for enough money to keep the company and the town afloat. I knew it wasn't my fault; he was the one who always wanted to spend more. I wanted for the people, but bought for them only what I was allotted. Still, Cleve kept attacking me, blaming me for his money problems, because I was such an easy target.

I tried to remind him that if only he had let me into his business matters, I could've helped. But that argument hardly made it past my lips before he'd stomp out of the room and slam the closest door, often times insulting me with hurtful words, some of them true, some not true at all.

I began to look forward to his business trips. Where before I missed him with a burning pang in my heart, I appreciated my time without him, and even dreaded his return. The staff and people of Redstone supported me emotionally while he was away, but there was just so much they could do with Cleve around. I still loved him, in my heart I knew I loved him deeply, but I became afraid of him. Then, when one of his business partners, Alfred Cass, died on Independence Day of a stroke, things really took a turn for the worse. Cleve was forced to sell the company to Mr. Gould and Mr. Rockefeller, and we quickly departed for Europe with plans to stay until the end of the year.

Cleve was strained the entire time, and it wasn't clear to me why we had to leave when he was always in communications with America. It made more sense for us to be back home, I thought. By then, I mostly kept my mouth closed. I questioned myself, what would come of adding my two cents? I'd only be berated, yelled at, ridiculed, and I had no energy anymore to combat his awful temper. It was better to go about my own business, which included pampering myself, shopping, dining, making small talk with other travelers and natives, and reading whatever I could get my hands on.

Three months into our trip overseas, around Thanksgiving time, another business partner, Julian Kebler, died of a brain hemorrhage. Then, three days later, Cleve's last remaining business partner, John Jerome, took his own life with a gun. Within five months, his three business partners were dead. It was a mess.

The boy gasps. "Did that really happen?" he asks.

"Which part?" I ask.

"About all three of his business partners dying within one year?"

"I'm afraid so," I answer.

"But that's crazy! Was there ever any kind of investigation?" the boys asks.

"What kind of investigation would there be? They all died in reasonable ways," I say.

"Reasonable ways? Sounds suspect to me," the boy says.

"Well, no one was going to risk their reputation and challenge the Almighty Cleve, if that's what you're suggesting," I answer, somewhat annoyed but aware that this young boy has a strong point, one I am sure many others had at the time. There was no evidence to show that Cleve had anything to do with these deaths, as coincidental as they may have seemed. "I don't really want to focus on this. Can I go on?" I ask.

"Yes, of course, I just thought it was so weird," he says.

"We all did," I say, looking in Manuele's direction, who offers me a nod of approval that all is fine, and that I should continue.

Those initial blissful days were long gone, and we were left strangers in the same home. I don't know how I stayed living there for seven more years; for as large as the house was, it wasn't large enough to contain the two of us. It was like I was already dead, even though I stayed busy every single day. I didn't want to frighten anyone with my pain, or cause anyone grief. I was determined to remain strong, and as much as Cleve tried to take all my strength for himself, I somehow was able to maintain my composure and my dignity. And my sanity.

Sucked into a long portal constructed of invisible webs, I find myself in a completely different space entirely. Far away from the children, far away from Manuele. Away from Redstone and the present.

I don't recognize this place at first because it is so jarring, but soon enough, I identify the darkened, crowded streets. People are moving around and through one another. Horse and wagons and fruit and vegetable vendors trample on the concrete ground, while the smell of manure permeates the smoky, thick air. Alongside the wooden carts are rows upon rows of black automobiles, fighting for their place, too.

I am in New York City, Manhattan. Buildings push against taller buildings. Staring straight up at the sky is the only relief. But the view of the sky is obscured also, with lines upon lines of drying laundry hanging from one tenement house to the next. There are sounds of people arguing, bargaining, children's laughing and running in the streets and chasing one another, old men and women shushing and punishing them, wandering dogs barking, firefighter sirens in the distance, and elevated trains rumbling along rickety tracks.

Black and grey smoke escapes past the skyline, billowing from rooftop chimneys. Pigeons gather in public spaces. Rats scurry in parking lots. Cockroaches hide in apartment corners.

Advertisements for soaps, political candidates, vehicles, cigarettes, furniture, clothes, tinctures, Broadway musicals, all are painted on faces of office buildings, leaving room only for condensed square windows. Flashbulb signage protrudes from restaurants, nightclubs, bars, stores, bakeries, butcher and candy shops. On and off, on and off, on and off. Words, words, words. If I look too closely I remember how my head would buzz like a bee's nest, the blood in my forehead veins would constrict, and my lungs would sting.

There is little room to think for one's self here. We are always being told what to think, what to want, what to buy, what to be. What to fear.

It's a different kind of life here. Alive in a way that the wilderness is not. Alive with humans and human endeavors. Nature has been pushed to the middle, pushed to Central Park where fancy ladies stroll arm-in-arm with fancy girlfriends or handsome loved ones; boulders double for lounge chairs; ponds carry rented rowboats; ornate stone tunnels house vagrants; mounds become sledding hills when it snows. In this city where thousands struggle everyday to get here, to live here, to make it here, nature is squeezed to the sidelines, to the dirtied rivers supporting foreign ships, to steel bridges where men lie buried inside from dying on the job, to manicured bushes and pink, yellow, and orange tulips sequestered between the two lanes of Park Avenue.

I look below and the city is outdoors now. I see myself, inside, solid as a board on a simple bed in a tiny room. A metal headboard frames the back of the mattress. The aging wallpaper's maroon-colored base hints at a hunter green leaf pattern. There is an oval, copper clock on the wall, and my eyes follow the seconds as they circle around and around and around the glass-covered white face with black, Roman numerals.

The air is tight as a vacuum; whatever air there is remains trapped inside me. It's my last breath. I keep it long in my lungs, to feel life in this body one last time. George Eliot's masterpiece *Middlemarch* is sprawled against my chest with my hands resting on the tattered hardcover book. My long, bony fingers are already cold.

I am here alone. There will be no one to find me but a hotel maid. Images of my earlier life in Redstone flash before me, almost as reflections on the clock ticking, ticking, ticking on the blank scene before me. I see the hodge-podge faces of the townspeople. There was not a place I could go in that town, or in the neighboring towns, where I could be anonymous. Everyone knew me. Even those I did not know knew me and greeted me. I read about myself in the local papers, and sometimes in the national papers. Photographs and paintings of me hung in many of the local establishments. Dignitaries came to visit us. They adored me. They praised me and asked me to play the piano for them, sing for them, ride horses with them, entertain them. Even when we visited New York and Chicago, we would inadvertently run into people we knew. Some were our friends, some our enemies, some gawkers, some haters. In many ways it was the life I had envisioned for myself when I was very young and felt trapped in Sweden. But the reality was such that the notoriety didn't feel at all like I thought it would. I thought it would feel nice, and it didn't at all.

We thought we were not alone because we were known. But deep within ourselves, both Cleve and I, we felt very, very alone. We couldn't find a common ground anymore. Our lives had become much too busy, much too complicated, too much everyone else's lives but our own. People saw in us what they wanted to see in us, until we no longer knew who we really were.

These are my last thoughts while in Alma's body. Such a popular woman I was in my youth, but there I lay, alone, with no one to hold my hand as I take my last breath. No one to tell me it will all be fine. No one to stroke my hair or touch my pale, wrinkled cheeks one last time. I am alone. All alone. I'm not sure how this happened, really, because it happened slowly, so very slowly over time. One decision at a time. One decision after another decision slowly but surely separating me from friends and family. Decisions to be separate. Decisions to cut myself off from all the other sides of me. Debilitating decisions that cut me from my very core, from my soul and my soul's desires.

I let the last breath go, I cannot hold it in any longer. It fills up the room, pushing molecules this way and that, the bigger molecules overrunning the smaller ones, until they creep out, jimmying out from under the door. I can see my body stiffen, almost instantaneously. It is left behind, minutes now from the air that once filled me.

I hover for a while longer until I fly off for the unknown. But I don't get too far. I am stuck in between two barriers. One is permeable, the other is not. I bang my energy against the impermeable barrier, but I can't get through, no matter how much I push. I push, push, push, until I am bumped back through the permeable barrier, and then before me are the towering arbors, emerald, pine, grass, fluorescent and pastel greens, every imaginable shade of green, green, green, green, bursting from heavy spring rains. Unstoppable rains. Enduring rains that bring life with them. The aspens are blooming, popping, waking, while the red canyons are stained black from the precipitation, like long happy tears falling down to the dense forests. Fluid white clouds are suspended between cliffs, redefining their outlines, creating new shapes in the landscape. Yellow dandelions carpet the lawns. Fat mushrooms sprout beside massive tree trunks. For miles. And miles and miles and miles.

I am home again. Yes, this is my home. I am home.

18

*T*his time the children don't realize that I have left, not even for a moment. For me the time away felt like an eternity, for them it was a nanosecond.

"We finally vacated the castle in 1911, and traveled regularly from Denver, New York and Europe," I say. "I left for France in 1915 from Denver, never to see Cleve again. Looking back, I'm not sure how that all happened, how I was able to leave his grip. It was a miracle really. I traveled between Paris, Denver, New York and Maryland, so no one was ever sure where I was at any given moment. When it was my time to die, I embraced it whole-heartedly. I was ready to go."

"But what happened to Cleve after you left?" Rose asks.

"I'm tired from all this memory-searching, my dear," I say.

"Maybe we could resume the story a little later?"

"Oh, but please, just a little more, Lady Bountiful," she says, "just a little more."

"Leave her be," Manuele says. "She's true to her word. *Signora* will finish the story at another time, Rose."

"It's okay," I reply. "I can go on for a little bit more. The girl's enthusiasm has given me some more energy."

I continue the story, trying my best to finish, or at least this portion of it, as quickly as possible:

With my spirit back in Redstone, I learned many things about Cleve, overhearing many conversations from locals. I learned that after Cleve and I had divorced, he found himself another wife, Lucille, in 1920. He married her in New York and eventually brought her to Redstone in 1924. They fixed up the castle, updating it for the current era; they kept a lot of people busy for a little while. Lucille was young, in her mid-twenties, while Cleve was in his seventies by then, and she took very good care of him until he died in his bedroom in the castle a couple of years later. As his wishes commanded, she spread his ashes all over the valley. He willed her everything, and soon after his passing, she remarried.

Lucille and her new husband squandered whatever money Cleve had left her; she burned all his papers and tried to turn the castle into a vacation destination. It didn't work. The timing was terrible, beginning with the stock market crash in 1929. By 1940, Lucille and her husband had sold off pieces of the buildings on the property and in town to different people, while selling other parts of the estate to scrap, like the southern gatehouse. Soon enough, she had sold the entire estate.

By the time my spirit returned to town in the late-1950s, the owner of the Hotel Colorado in Glenwood Springs had bought the castle. It was the first and only time I revisited the castle; it was under such construction, I worried for its sustainability, and decided never to go back. I was lucky enough not to encounter Cleve then, not sure if he was alive or dead at that point, in Redstone or beyond.

"Where did you die?" the boy asks.

"In a hotel room, as an old lady, in New York City. The year was 1955," I respond coldly, fresh from my recent travels to that lonely day.

"You must have had a huge funeral," Rose says.

"I actually died all alone, sweetheart. I ended my life pretty much alone," I say. "By then, I had let people lose track of me."

"But how is that possible?" Rose asks incredulously. "You were so popular!"

"Popularity is not love. Popularity just means that a lot of people know your name and your face and some things you've done, but it doesn't mean that those admirers really know you. When you no longer represent what other people want you to be, they have little use for you," I say to the girl. She twists up her face at me, bewildered.

"But, but, you were so loved, you did so much for other people, you were so beautiful," Rose says then bursts into tears.

"Oh, dear, it's okay." I comfort her, wishing I could touch her, too. The best I can do in my amorphous state is swirl my good energy around her, creating a hurricane of light that engulfs her bright orange aura.

"Only a handful of people truly love you for who you are. Figure out who those people are because those are the people who will be there for you when it's your time to go," I say.

This news unsettles the girl. She doesn't know what to do with this conflicting information. The boy rubs her back gently until she stops crying. She wipes away her tears with her palms, rubs her eyes, and takes a deep breath.

"Can you go on with your story?" Rose asks in a sniffled voice. "I'm very sorry I got so upset. I didn't expect that to happen."

"It's fine, dear. Better you understand these things when you're younger. I wish I had. Okay, now, where were we?"

"You were talking about the castle," Manuele reminds me, about what happened after we were all gone, when you came back after your death."

"Oh, yes, thank you, thank you," I say. "Well, the new owner wanted to turn the castle into an all-season resort, adding a new wing to the building, as well as an enclosed swimming pool and tennis courts. He converted the front lawn into a golf course, and the northern gatehouse into a ski lodge after building a ski lift on the property. Aspen, just fifty miles away by car, was becoming a premiere ski town by then, and he wanted to jump on its lucrative bandwagon. But in the midst of all these rejuvenating plans, the new owner died in 1960. I was not the least bit surprised. After learning that Cleve had been dead many years and was supposedly haunting the castle, I suspected his spirit was just not going to let all these changes happen without his consent. Especially when the new owner paid no attention to the various warning signs, not believing in spirits at all.

"The property changed hands many, many times after that, but no one could hold onto it for very long. Cleve is going to hold onto that castle for as long as he can. He has an ego like no one I have ever known before. He hates having to let anything go, the way he had to let his company go to Mr. Rockefeller, and the castle, abandoning it for all those years, and how he eventually had to let me go, too."

"Why's he like that?" the boy asks. "Why was he such a difficult person?"

"Well, I have my own theories regarding your question, but there are some obvious reasons why," I say. "Why are you so interested in that?" I ask, curious as to why such a young boy would wonder about the psychology of an old man he never knew.

"I know so little about my own beginning, about my birth parents. I wonder how much I am like them, how much of me comes from them, and how much comes from my life here. I'm often interested in what makes people who they are, what makes them do what they do and be who they are," he says with a kind of confidence that's new to me.

"It is curious, isn't it?" I say. "Now that I am in this phase of my awareness, I wonder how much of our past lives make up who we are in each current life. Most of us don't remember anything about our past lives, but that doesn't mean they don't affect us in many ways."

Not wanting to disappoint the children, I share some more about Cleve, like how he was an orphan at a young age, and no one ever took care of him. He always had to take care of himself. He pushed his way through the world.

I knew very little of Cleve's early history; no one really knew much about his past, especially before he started making a lot of money. I do know he was born on March 6, 1851 in Brooklyn, New York. He had an older brother and younger sister, and their mother died when they were all very small.

When he was six years old, Cleve went to live in Iowa with

his dad, who two years later sent him to live with relatives in Rhode Island, where he started school. By fourteen, he had left home to go to work on his own at a cotton mill, and then when he was sixteen, he moved to New York City to work and go to night school. Three years later, at nineteen years old, he returned back to Iowa to work at a fuel company, which he eventually took over when he was twenty-six. Five years later a railroad company sent him to Colorado to investigate how much coal was in the area, and that began his long love affair with the state.

Colorado had only become an official American state less than five years before Cleve first visited. He traveled to every mine in the state, and soon knew more about the coal business with a greater vision for the future than anyone else in the country, or so he related to me.

I remember Cleve's going on and on about how much he loved Colorado. How he felt it was his, all his for the taking. At first I admired his passion for the land, his strong sense of self, but soon enough his conceit bothered and later scared me.

I tell them about Cleve's impressive background, how both of his parents were born into illustrious families. His father was a descendent of Samuel Osgood, the first U.S. Postmaster General since the forming of the Constitution. Samuel Osgood had an impressive political career, and was close friends with George Washington. When New York City was the seat of the United States Federal Government before relocating to Washington, DC, it was Samuel Osgood's home in downtown Manhattan that became the official residence for the first President of the United States. On Cleve's mother's side descended the twenty-second and the twenty-fourth United States President, Grover Cleveland, who was Cleve's cousin. So even though Cleve felt disconnected from his family, I tell them, he knew he came from good stock.

"Your father must have loved that about him!" the girl exclaims.

"He did," I reply. "How do you know that?"

"Well, you said earlier how much your father admired the American Founding Fathers," she says.

"You listen very well," I say. "You must do very well in school, both of you."

Both children nod their heads.

"Can I ask you a personal question?" she asks me.

"Has this not been personal so far?" I ask, teasing them. "Yes, please, what is it you want to know?"

"You and Mr. Osgood, you never had any children, did you?" the girl asks.

"No, we didn't," I answer curtly, surprised it was such a personal question after all.

"Why not?" she wants to know.

Manuele tries to quiet her, not wanting to upset me, but I answer her question more openly this time. "Although he never talked about it, Cleve was embarrassed that he never had children. I think he blamed all three of his wives for our infertility, but we all knew it was him. He wasn't a very affectionate man, always so busy with business and making money and trying to control the entire world, he cared very little for romance. But even when there was romance, there still were never any children. It made me sad for a while, but looking back I was very grateful. There's no way Cleve would've let me go with his children in tow, even if he wouldn't have enjoyed them, or known what to do with them. He would have considered his children property, his possessions. He wasn't the fathering type. He never had a childhood, and so he could never relate to children. He considered them afterthoughts."

"But did you want children?" she asks me.

"Yes, of course," I say honestly. But that wasn't going to be part of Alma's fate. I really did love shopping for the children in the neighborhood. It was some of the best fun I ever had. Visiting all those wonderful toy stores in New York and Chicago. The wooden puppets were my favorite; they were painted with such sweet faces and bright colors that I bought enough of them for a hundred puppet theatres. I even wrote a few songs on my piano for the school puppet shows.

Cleve had trouble just sitting through one of those shows. In fact, I am sure he never actually saw more than ten minutes of any of them. You can imagine why a young woman like me was so taken with him, though. Did I really have a choice in the matter? I ask the children, while also asking myself.

"There are so many stories I could tell you about Cleve. He was larger than life itself. And now he's larger than death. How do we move on from him? How do we free Redstone from his grip? I have been wondering this for as long as I can remember now," I say.

I look at the children closely. I see how innocently they love each other. I see how pure their love for each other is, and how open they are to everything. I don't ever want to stop seeing that goodness in their eyes and in their hearts. But by this point, I am ready to leave them for a little while. I don't want to engage in any more questions, and tell them so.

Weary from my memories, I need to be as free as I can from them for a bit, which might sound strange coming from a spirit, but the thing of it is, I still have my consciousness. I carry it with me always; my consciousness is, in fact, what and who I am, nothing more and nothing less. And whether I am in a body or floating above it, or beyond the trappings of the Earth's gravitational energy, I am still my consciousness. And my consciousness heightens with every experience, every life, I have.

Communicating with the children, however, makes me realize that I am truly ready to move on. I am ready to let go of Cleve and Redstone. I am ready to move on to my next journey. It's no good staying here for too much longer. I know the town's paralyzed, too, while I hover around it.

I float away into the clouds, and wave through the wind. My spirit glides with the birds and catches leaves as they fall from the trees. Encircling the cool air, I feel other spirits all around me. I don't know many of them, but we know we are here together. Some are newer, some older. Some are happy to be here, some want to escape as fast as they can. Sometimes the spirits clash and turn into clapping thunderstorms. But sometimes we spin around together and bring comfort from the hot, blazing sun. Sometimes we do nothing at all, and let the nights and early mornings be still. Sometimes we stir up the clouds and make them cry.

Today, the breeze comes and goes, and the river flows with ease. We are collectively undecided.

19

The children, Manuele and I make a plan to go to the castle. Manuele communicates that he will accompany me all the way. The children make arrangements with Patricia, the castle's keeper, for our visitation. They disclose the complete truth to her, and having experienced the spirits herself, Patricia approves their request. She asks to be a witness and we all agree; she is a believer, which is our only requirement. The castle is more her home than anyone else's at this point anyway.

It's winter by now and the road to the castle from the Redstone Inn is covered in thick snow. The night before brought a storm, leaving the pine tree branches draped in white.

The children's boots make fresh tracks alongside some deer and elk hoof-prints. The robins sing in their high-pitched voices, welcoming us. The river's still warm enough to flow; the power of the mountain snowmelt pushes the current along, preventing most of the water from freezing. The rocks, like salt-and-pepper shakers, create meandering pathways for the river to ramble. I remember so well walking down that mile-long road on chilly and clear days, breathing in the crisp air, opening my lungs, renewing me for the challenges ahead.

Many of the servants' homes aligning the walk are in much lesser condition than they used to be, but the white firehouse and striking irongate have retained their splendor. The olive green paint and red roofs are new, as is a white pipe running down the front of the castle, but there's no denying the local maroon sandstone, reflecting the towering red cliffs across the river.

Throughout the walk, I feel Manuele close by me, hovering over the children, using their energy for courage. The closer I near the castle, the stronger I can feel Cleve's pull. I can't tell whether or not he recognizes my essence, but the attraction feels stronger than ever, and I let it suck me into its rough embrace.

It's odd seeing the castle this way, barren without human life, no music seeping out from the windows or from the lawn, no servants shoveling snow, no carriage horses awaiting passengers, no rushed voices from newly arrived guests, no noise but a sudden crash of a snow shelf sliding from the roof, making the entire building seem like a mausoleum. In the courtyard, one of my green stagecoaches is on display, as immobile as a carcass.

We arrive at the entrance to the castle, crowding the impending front door made of nutmeg-colored wood with black iron, which decorates the stained-glass window with swirls, spheres and a central tassel. We know that once we open this door, there is no going back.

A small, red fox appears as if from nowhere, making himself comfortable between the girl's feet and a pile of snow. She kneels down to pet him, and soon enough he scampers back a few hundred paces, holding his body high, also awaiting the upcoming scene.

The children grab each other's gloved hands tightly. They knock on the imposing door. We hear a quick, hard turn with the key, and then the heavy door opens inward. I miss hearing the large bell ring outside, which a footman would pull, letting the butler know someone was calling.

The children step into the entrance first, working hard not to make a sound. They take off their coats, hats and gloves quickly, and hold them over their forearms, shocked from the strong, sudden heat emanating from within. Soon enough they notice the photograph of me in my riding habit (a lady's top hat and suit), which hangs on the hand-stenciled linen wallpaper decorated with pineapples and angels. They look back and forth at me as if to make the comparison from then to now. I seem so serious in that photograph that it makes me chuckle, but for the most part, my present spirit looks almost identical to the photograph.

Patricia takes their winter coverings and places them over the stair railing, where another long, black coat already rests.

The children, with Patricia close behind, head towards the Great Hall.

Without anyone uttering a single word yet, there he is, a distinct and familiar spirit, his back towards the windows, his overgrown belly facing the group.

The children stop short, breathing in deeply, surprised at how surprised they really are.

Standing before us is Cleve, all 5'4" of him, blond hair parted in the center, with a full blond mustache to match, and blue eyes piercing through the darkness.

The children exhale as deeply as they had inhaled. Patricia watches the children's every move as clues for her own reactions. Cleve is wearing the same British tailored white tie tuxedo he wore the day we met at King Leopold's palace in Belgium. He is naturally smoking a foreign cigar with his left hand. I almost wouldn't recognize him any other way.

"Alma," he says immediately, "It's nice to see you."

"Well, then, are you going to be nice to me now that I'm finally here?" I ask coyly.

"I wasn't always nice?" he asks.

I laugh at him. "I wouldn't say so."

He grimaces.

"We had many fun times together, don't you remember, my dear?" he asks.

"I remember, but I also remember all the fighting, the screaming, the tension," I say.

"We never fought. It was everyone else I fought with, but not with you," he says.

"That's very convenient for you to remember it that way," I say.

"Well, who do we have here with you?" Cleve asks, changing the subject before the conversation becomes too intimate.

"You remember Manuele, don't you?" I inquire.

"Your pet project?" he asks sarcastically.

"My friend," I answer, correcting him. "My best student."

"And who are the children? The caretaker I know too well, but these children I have never encountered before. I sense they can see us, no?"

"Yes, they can," I reply. "They're the reason I'm here."

"And how's that?"

"They sought me out, and gave me the courage to finally confront you."

"Confront me? With what? I'm already dead," he says.

"So, you realize you're dead?"

"Of course I realize I'm dead. What kind of inane question is that? How could I not know I'm dead?" he says, in that condescending voice I know all too well.

"Because not all spirits realize they are dead. It certainly took me awhile," I say.

"That's idiocy. I know I'm dead. I figured that out pretty quickly, especially when Lucille moved in here with her new husband. I was dead only ten minutes, and another man was sleeping in my bed," he says.

"She must've been with him before then," I say.

"I'd say so," Cleve says with a smirk on his face.

"You do have a lot of trouble moving on," I say.

"Well, where in God's name do you think I'm supposed to move on to? I'm dead. I thought we already established that. And this is my castle."

"*Our* castle," I say, correcting him.

"It was ours, until you left. Said you couldn't spend one more minute in my presence. Said you needed to go off and save the world. Said you were better than me."

"I never said I was better than you," I say.

"Well, you sure acted like it," he responds, his voice sounding like a small child's.

"These matters shouldn't haunt the castle anymore, though. Why should we ruin everyone else's future too?" I ask.

"This is my town. Always was, always will be," he says.

"How can I convince you to pass onto the other side?" I ask, almost pleading.

"I'm not going anywhere," he says.

"There must be something I can do to get you there," I say.

"I said: I'm not going anywhere," he repeats himself.

"Please consider leaving, Cleve. For everyone's sake," I say, and detest how my voice sounds when it's begging.

Cleve thinks for a while, adding up the possibilities. Until he finally answers, "Well, yes, there is something you can do to get me to leave."

"And what is that?" I ask.

"Be my wife again," he says.

"That's impossible," I say.

"Well, then, I'll never leave this place," he says.

The girl moves forward after listening very attentively during the entire conversation. "How about in your next lives?" she asks.

"Our next lives?" Cleve and I both say together.

"Yes," she says. "You told us that souls go through many lives, right Mrs. Osgood? So, in the next one, maybe you two could be together again."

Patricia only hears the girl's response since she's not able to see or hear Cleve and me, even though I sense she can slightly detect our energy. She says to the children, "You know, I have heard of such a thing, a soul contract. It's when one soul makes a promise with another soul for the next life. To work out problems that weren't settled in their previous lives."

"Very interesting," Cleve says. "Well, then, let's do a soul contract together, Alma."

"Oh, I don't think I could manage another life with you, with all due respect, my love."

"Yes, you could," Cleve says. "If our identities were different, you could."

"But you would never agree to being anything less than you were," I say.

"Yes, I would, if it meant we could have a life together again. A good life this time."

"Nothing fancy," I say.

"Nothing too fancy," Cleve says.

There's a long silence.

"How can we be sure that this soul contract even works?" Cleve says directly to the girl. "Ask the caretaker how we can be sure before I get tricked into passing over and losing Alma forever."

The girl repeats the recent exchange to Patricia, to which Patricia replies, "I think there has to be something deeper to it than just wanting to be married again. There is something new that must be learned in the new forms, because the whole purpose of relationships is to teach you something new, to elevate your awareness until you fully become love."

"I don't even know what that means!" Cleve yells. "That makes absolutely no sense. To fully become love. What a joke!"

"Which is exactly why you are still roaming these hallways," I say. "I just can't imagine contracting my soul to yours, and living with you all over again."

"I will promise to give you children this time," he says.

"You told me it was my fault."

"C'mon," Cleve says. "We knew that was a lie."

"So, you knew all along it was you?" I ask, incredulously.

"How could it not have been me? Three wives and no children? Not even one pregnancy," he says.

"All the lies, the stories, I was so tired of it. How you deflected your anger onto everyone else, blamed us all for your unhappiness, when all along-" I begin to say.

"Not all along," Cleve says. "I've had some time to consider things here in this, in this, what do you call this, this-" he says, waving his arms about.

"I call it the Middle World," I reply.

"I think there's another word for it, but it eludes me now," he says.

"Returning to the point," I say, "tell me again why I would promise to live another life with you?"

"To save all these poor people, to free them from our madness," he answers, trying to appeal to my higher self.

"How you use my good will against me! That's just not fair!" I scream.

"It is fair. You left me when I was sick in bed for over a week, when I was defenseless and unable to stop you. No one told me you were gone. By then you were untraceable. How fair was that? I almost lost my mind that first year without you!"

"I'm sorry," I say. "I didn't know what else to do."

"I'm not a monster," he says.

"I never said you were."

"You didn't have to say it."

"We're fighting again, Cleve. We can't go through a whole other lifetime of this," I say.

"We may have to just to get past it," he says. "Before we can move on."

It strikes me then. That's it. I must be his wife again. I really have no choice. At that moment Patricia somehow intuitively understands our dispute.

"You know," Patricia says to the children. "They don't have to come back as husband and wife. Or with her as female and he as male. The relationship could be familial, or even as very close friends, or peers."

"And who decides what the relationship is then?" I ask, very intrigued. Maybe this can happen, maybe this can be possible, for better or worse, just as we had vowed to one another so many years ago.

The girl repeats the question for Patricia.

"Well, that's the Divine at work, I believe. I don't think we can determine the form and shape of the relationship, but I don't really know for sure. This is not my expertise," Patricia answers. "But I suspect it's all about what it is you want to learn in the next life. What you believe your soul needs to experience in order to grow."

"What is it you'd want to learn, Mrs. Osgood?" the girl asks me.

I contemplate her question for a moment. I imagine how Cleve will play a role in this learning.

"I want to learn to accept love that is kind and benevolent, not harsh and dominating. I don't think I knew how to accept that kind of love before. Maybe I never wanted to take so much responsibility, or maybe I just didn't think I could," I say, learning something new about myself just by speaking it out loud. "And you, Cleve?" I ask him directly.

"I want to know what it means to have a family. A good and simple family," Cleve responds with more humility than I've ever recognized in him before.

"Is any family really simple?" the boy turns to ask the girl just above a whisper.

"I don't know, but I'd like to find out," Cleve says, indirectly responding to the boy's question.

"Must we be human then?" I ask, trying my best not to disturb Cleve's sudden vulnerability, while also keeping his anger from rising to the surface.

Again the girl translates for Patricia, to which Patricia answers: "I told you, this is not my expertise."

"But how do we even make this soul contract in the first place? How do we make it so, regardless of the specifics?" This time the boy reiterates Cleve's question for Patricia.

Patricia says in a short tone, "I don't know anymore than I've already shared." She doesn't seem to like being deaf to spirit-talk, but if she were born with the ability to hear us, she wouldn't have lasted living in the castle for as long as she has; I'm sure she would have gone mad a long time ago.

We all stand still in utter silence. It is a very good question: how can we initiate this soul contract? To allow us out of this Middle World and into a higher one, so that we can return once again to Earth in other physical bodies?

Manuele moves closer to Cleve and me, making his presence better known. He has a wish of his own, too, and I have a pretty good feeling what it is.

In an instant, I feel myself return to my and Cleve's last train ride out of Redstone more than a century ago, far away from the present gathering. Cleve and I are arriving at the train depot after a carriage ride, jostled this way and that, the large, wooden wheels shaking with such force that we are vibrating along with them. The yellow aspen leaves set the landscape ablaze; the tall, chalk-white tree trunks with knotty eyes peer into our very souls, making the entire valley proud like soldiers going off to war.

Once on the *Sunrise* private train car, I follow the autumn paradise, imagining the crisp air against my face, hoping to burn the images into my brain to endure the rest of my life. Mighty Mount Sopris carries some new snow on its peak, like a fifty-year old man whose beard has just begun to age. The red cliffs reach for the heavens, each precipice aiming higher than its neighbor. The Crystal River canyon opens to fields of green and hay, cows and horses, minding their own business, drinking from the translucent, sparkling water.

Cleve and I hardly say a word to each other throughout this last united ride to Carbondale, although I think Cleve is mumbling something resentful under his breath. He is too distracted, reading a *New York Times* and the first *Camp & Plant* newsletter on his lap, to succumb to the breathtaking scenery. He puffs on his cigar when he isn't curling the end of his mustache. His smoke mirrors the coal exhaust emanating from the train, greying the sky in its midst. It is obvious Cleve believes he'll return to Redstone one day. I want to cry, but the tears won't come.

Outside the train car, two bald eagles dance in their flight, teasing me with their freedom and joy. One day, I say to myself, one day, I will be just as free as the eagles are here.

I read the front page of the faded and brittle ten year old *Camp & Plant* newsletter. It has become Cleve's talisman. He takes it with him wherever he goes; I think to prove that his dream once came true, that it wasn't all imagined. I read the words on the cover of the first issue, Volume 1, Issue 1, published on December 14, 1901:

> To bring the various coal and iron camps clos-
> er together and to promote the work of the
> Sociological Department are the objects of "Camp

and Plant." The effort to cover the field of this weekly is entirely new and for this reason and because of the unique methods to be employed it will not conflict with any other paper and at the same time will supply a present need.

There are thirty-eight camps, rolling-mills and steel works of the Colorado Fuel and Iron Company in Colorado, Wyoming and New Mexico, at which fifteen thousand men, representing seventy-five thousand people, are employed in digging coal and iron ore and making it into coke, iron and steel.

It is this accomplishment that gratified Cleve's ambition more than any other feat: employing all those people, controlling thousands, being so very important. Without loving parents, he believed conquering the world from a new land with new magic would conquer his unrelenting feelings of loss and pain. But no matter how backbreaking the transformation of fossils into fuel may be, it pales in comparison to the work needed to transform anger into love.

By the time we board the train at Glenwood Springs for Denver, the dark clouds have moved in with a thunderclap accompanied by hard, pounding rain to echo my sadness.

"Alma, Alma!" I hear Cleve yell at me. "Will you come back here this instant? We are trying to make some very important decisions here, and there you go, disappearing into the clouds again."

I return to the consortium at the castle. The children and Manuele expect an answer from me. But how am I to know what to do next? I don't know anyone who can help us with this so-called soul contract, with helping us to pass onto the other side. Why are they all looking to me as if I am the only one who has all these answers? If I knew how to return to the other side and stay there, I would have done so a long time ago.

We soon agree that the answer will come to one of us, and that we will remain open until the answer arrives. We have faith that the person who can help us will make him or herself known when the time is right, no matter how anxious we are to close this chapter of our existence.

The children return to their homes while Manuele and I decide to stay in the castle with Cleve. My hope is that once we all leave the castle, we will never enter again. I resolve to enjoy my old home this one last time.

Patricia dutifully stays in the castle with us. Cleve tries to reconcile with me, but the feelings I used to have for him are gone, no matter how much I try to bring back the amorous emotions, infatuation, really, I once had for him. My heart has turned away from him, lost for what feels like forever. I wish that we didn't have to live another life together, but at this point, I'm not sure how to get out of that arrangement either.

Manuele is very adoring, as usual. His love grows even stronger for me, but I cannot reciprocate with him, or with Cleve, especially in our current spirit-states. As we are now, Manuele is still a young, innocent boy to me. Any romantic feelings for him just feel wrong.

We all wait for a sign, for hope of transformation, whatever, whenever it will be. We surrender to the unknown, as there is no truer way to be.

20

One early spring day, I see a horde of people enter the castle. The snowpack outside is thinner and muddy-brown in parts, as the warmer air melts away the harshest residue of winter. A fleet of vans and giant vehicles fill the parking lot.

The visitors move around from one room to the other, speaking quickly and loudly. There are oversized hand-held machines, endless artificial lights, rows of cheap chairs and clipboards everywhere.

A handsome middle-aged man stomps into the Great Hall. His sudden and dramatic entrance calls my attention. He puts his hands on his hips then waves them around in the air.

"Chris! Chris!" the man yells.

"What is it?" an older man responds, running into the Great

Hall, a bulky apparatus strapped around the circumference of his head. I have certainly seen this man before.

"There are people here," the handsome man says, moving his body back and forth.

"Of course there are, Jack," the older man says. "We're filming today."

Yes, I remember now, he is the man who was inspecting the Inn, the one who thought my portrait was beautiful.

"That's not what I mean," the man called Jack whines. "I can feel spirits in here."

"You mean ghosts?" the director Chris asks.

"Yes," Jack states. "I heard there were ghosts in here, but I didn't believe it until now."

"What makes you so sure it's true now?" Chris demands, exasperated.

"I don't know, but I know. And I won't do any work in here until they're gone," Jack announces.

"Jack, we don't have time for this. We're on a very tight budget, and a very tight schedule."

"I don't care," Jack argues. "I will not work in here with all these spirits. It's bad luck. If we don't fix this problem now, the whole film will be ruined."

This problem? I repeat to myself. We're a problem? Who does this man think he is? What a fool!

"Who can help us with this problem?" Jack demands.

"One minute," Chris replies, walking away. I hear him whisper "Actors, actors!" under his breath. I follow him. He is looking for someone. He wanders around the main level of the castle until he finds her.

"Patricia," Chris says to her. "I know this may sound strange, if you knew actors you might not think it so weird, but regardless, the lead actor says he, he, detects ghosts in this castle, and, um, he says he won't work with them here. Do you have any idea how we can deal with this? I'm at a loss. I don't care if you make something up. I don't believe he even knows what he's talking about anyway."

Patricia smiles. "Well, it's true, there are spirits here."

"Bull nuggets!" Chris exclaims.

"Excuse me?" Patricia responds, taken off-guard. "If you don't believe me then-"

"Sorry, it's something my five year-old boy says, and I've kind of adopted it."

"Well, I don't think your son can help us with this. But there may be someone who can, though, if you're interested, that is," Patricia says snidely.

"I am," Chris replies apologetically. "I am."

"The problem is that I don't know who that person is, and I don't feel right asking around because it may not go so well in the town. We once had someone try to do a clearing here, but it made no difference. Also, the current owner doesn't want to hear any word of ghosts in the castle, and this is a small valley; word travels fast and far here. But I'm sure it would be okay if you look around for one, if you're kind of quiet about it."

"And how would I do that?" asks Chris. "This is not exactly what I signed up for when I took on this directing job," he says, complaining. "I've given into some crazy requests from actors, but this one is definitely the craziest."

"I'm not sure how you'd find exactly who you're looking for, but I've heard there are several mediums and psychics in this valley who can clear ghosts. You'll have better access to these clairvoyants than I would considering your line of work, I'd imagine," Patricia says.

"Really? You think so?" the director says in a nasty voice, shaking his head to the ceiling.

"I'm sorry," Patricia says. "I wish I could help you, but I just can't."

It occurs to me then that maybe Patricia doesn't want us gone. Maybe she doesn't like the idea of our going to the other side? Maybe Cleve is really wanted here as much as he wants to be here?

The director stomps off and returns to speaking with the sensitive actor.

"You're absolutely sure you can't work with these ghosts?" the director says, pressuring Jack. "Perhaps they're friendly?"

"No, I just don't trust them," Jack says.

You don't trust us? I think. What's not to trust? I feel possessive of the castle now. I'm not sure I want to leave it in their hands, not sure they should get the right to capture it in their offensively giant cameras.

"Okay, fine then, we'll have to find some kind of medium, a psychic, clairvoyant, whatever you call them, like the caretaker says. She says we have to find one ourselves. She can't help us. Do you have any idea where to find one? Because I don't have a clue," Chris says.

"Of course. I have a very good friend in Malibu. She's very talented, but she's also very busy, but if we pay all her expenses to get here and stay here, I'm sure she'll come," Jack says.

"She's very busy?" the director says sardonically. "There's a lot of work for clearing ghosts these days?"

"Where've you been hiding?" Jack says. "She's ten times busier than I am."

Patricia joins the director and actor in their conversation, seemingly unsure of what role she should be playing in all this planning. "There is a stipulation," Patricia says. "When you find your medium and bring her here, you can't be in or around the castle while she works."

"Why is that?" the director asks.

"Because," Patricia states, "that's the only way it'll work."

"Then how will we know that the ghosts are gone for good?" the actor asks.

"I'd assume you'd know since you're the one who sensed them in the first place," she answers.

I am impressed by Patricia's quick responses. She's pretty astute. Maybe we should just let her stay in the castle and keep her company.

"Well, that is true," the actor says.

"And since I overheard that the medium is your friend, she'll be able to tell you, too. That is, if you trust her," Patricia says off-handedly.

"Well, there's no reason to be so, so rude about it." The actor berates Patricia.

"I'm sorry. Was I being rude? I didn't mean to be," she replies, still a little rudely.

The director laughs under his breath.

"I'm not going to work in a hostile environment, period," the actor warns. "With or without ghosts."

"Settle down," Chris the director says. "It's all going to be fine." He turns to Patricia.

"Thank you for all your help, Patricia. We'll let you know when the medium arrives, and we can go from there. We'll stay away until her work is done."

"Thank you," Patricia says.

"We really do appreciate your help," Chris says. "And for letting us film here. This is a magnificent castle, with an amazing history. I can see why the ghosts want to make their home here."

Well, at least the director's waking up, I think. Whether he believes in us or not, he's doing a better job of pretending now. And poor Patricia, she really doesn't want things to change. But honestly, how many people really ever do? Perhaps I don't either, even if I know that's what's best.

I thank the Universe for having directed us to this medium in the most unexpected of ways.

21

*S*he has dark skin with round, chocolate brown eyes. Her black, wavy hair rolls down her back. She wears a burnt orange shawl that covers most of her front. She sits in the library, on the floor, legs crossed. Patricia and the children stand in the Great Hall, behind the line that separates the two rooms. She calls herself Chipeta.

She beckons Cleve, Manuele and me to her. She approaches Cleve and me first.

"This castle is the home you two built together. It is a manifestation of your life and your love. It is a legacy, but it's of the material world and has no place in the spiritual realm. It's the spiritual realm you need to enter into, where you need to return. Why do you think you are resisting a place of peace?"

Her voice is clean and even, but melodic, too.

"This is my home. I can't leave," Cleve announces. He is the first one to communicate with Chipeta directly.

"Do you believe you are this home, then? That there is nothing beyond the material world for you?"

"I don't believe, period," he says, being difficult on purpose.

"But can you see the long tunnel, with the light at the end? Do you see it?"

"Perhaps," Cleve says.

"You realize you can go there, and be free?" Chipeta says.

"No, I don't want to," Cleve says, as if we haven't already resolved this.

"You don't want to be free?" she asks.

"I don't want to lose my connection to Alma," he says quietly.

"You won't. She will be in the spirit world, too. Your relationship cannot be healed any more during this incarnation. You must start anew for it to grow."

Cleve consider this proposition, spinning around to view his castle one last time as John Cleveland Osgood.

"I am afraid I will miss my home too much," he says.

"Once you pass over, you won't be able to feel loss or loneliness. There's no such thing there. You will never be alone there, you are never alone, you do not possess anything, and nothing possesses you. It is only on Earth and in your current state that you can feel the pain from loss and loneliness."

"Then why would I ever leave the other side once I've passed over?" he asks, genuinely curious.

"Because you want your soul to grow. You want new experiences. You can't remember, or truly feel, how much pain you felt on Earth once you are on the other side; it's like being in an infinite dream, or an abstract idea. You are no longer connected to Earth in that emotional or physical way," she explains. "Earth is like a school where your soul can learn. And when it is time for your soul to learn more, you return to Earth."

"Okay, then," he says. "If you promise."

"It's not a promise I can make," she says. "It's part of the laws of our universe." She pauses and I can tell he is seriously contemplating his decision. "Do you see the light? Just let yourself be moved towards it, and you will become part of it. Alma will follow soon after."

And with that, Cleve gazes upon me as if he is drowning, and then allows himself to be pulled into the tunnel, through the light. A heaviness slips out of the window, dissipating like a bad odor that's been set free.

I know it is my turn next.

"Alma," she says. "Do you know why you are still here?"

"Because of Cleve, his energy keeps me stuck here," I answer.

"But if that were the case, wouldn't you be gone by now? Wouldn't you have passed on as soon as he did?" she asks.

"I suppose," I respond, coyly.

"Do you know why you are still here?" she asks me again.

I think some more about this bewildering question, and then it hits me like summer hail. "It must be that I want to be here, too!"

"Yes," she says. "It has been your choice all along to be here. You placed the blame on Cleve, but you were just as responsible. You could've left at any time, but you chose to return to Redstone, you chose to stay away from the castle yet still be near it, and now you are choosing to let go. Do you see the light now?"

I look out the window. There is a bright orb of white light. I can feel its pull on me, a slight tug, warm and womb-like.

"Are you ready to go there now?" Chipeta asks.

"It would be nice, to not feel so trapped," I say.

"Then go," she says. "It's as easy as just allowing yourself to move towards the light."

"I have one more question," I say.

"Yes," Chipeta replies in a loving voice. "You may ask me as many questions as you'd like. Until you are ready to go, I am here."

"Okay, thank you," I say. "I want to know if I have to live another life with Cleve, if I don't want to."

"That's up to you, Alma. It's all what you want, what you feel you need to do in order to evolve," she answers.

"But I promised him," I say.

"Did you?" she asks.

"Well, sort of, but not completely. It was more his idea, what he needed to hear to pass on from here," I say.

"Well, then, that's his issue, the energy that he must deal with. He cannot force you to do anything you don't want to do, especially on the other side. That will become clearer to him once he is settled there. You will see. You will be able to talk to him about it more easily there," Chipeta explains.

"I will?" I ask desperately. "Because I really don't feel like I'm up for the task of living with him on Earth again."

"Then don't. Don't criticize what you want and what you don't want," Chipeta tells me.

"But I feel like I tricked him then, which will make him very angry," I say fretfully.

"You didn't trick him. It's what he wanted, what he needed to hear. And he won't be angry with you. There is no anger on the other side. Only love. You have nothing to fear there," she says, reassuring me.

"Nothing?" I ask, wanting so much to believe her.

"Nothing," she says. "Because I have tapped into the One, the Source of Everything, through this life. I've lived throughout this country, and in India for many years, studying, praying, learning, knowing. I carry with me the knowledge of my Native American and my African ancestors."

I am studying her. There is a richness behind her eyes, and yet something else foreign to me also lives there. There's a part of me that can relate to her completely, and yet another part that cannot at all.

"You have the choice to trust me or not," Chipeta says. "I cannot convince you of anything. It is your choice to trust, to believe in what I am saying. If it feels right to you, trust in it. If not, do not trust, and wait for a time when you'll know better, when you can trust better in the healing laws of the universe."

"No, I want to go now. I want to believe now," I say, but then I hesitate. "But, but, what about all these people who want to film here? I'm not sure I want them here."

"Why not?" she asks me.

"I'm not sure they'll appreciate it like they should," I say.

"And so you will stay behind to keep holding onto what is not yours?" she questions me gently. "You haven't seemed to mind letting go of it until this very moment."

"Yes, because I knew Cleve was here, protecting it, saving it for us," I explain. This revelation is new to me. Before this moment, I had no idea it belonged to me.

"Why not open up the castle for other people? You have

always been a generous person. Perhaps when the castle is freed from past energies it will be able to provide new energy for other people's journeys?" Chipeta says.

I like this idea. I have loved being a generous person. It is one of my best traits. I don't want to lose it now, not when I have come this far.

"I think I'm ready now," I say, surrendering.

"Are you sure?" she asks.

"Yes, I am sure," I respond with fortitude.

"I will send you with love and light then," Chipeta says. "Remember, you have the choice. You have always had the choice."

I take a moment and feel deeply into myself. Something inside of me tells me she is speaking the truth. I am ready, I tell myself. Yes, I am ready. I say goodbye to the children. I tell Manuele I will see him again soon. I thank Chipeta. I thank her profusely. I am ready. Yes, I am ready. It's time for me to move on, to take the next leg of this soul's journey.

And so it is. I shoot up like a column of light as soon as I make the decision to free myself. I zoom through the light at staggering speed. Free from the material world, I feel good and clean, easy and correct. Stabilized somehow, even within the lightning speed.

There's a strong sense of relief. There isn't any tension, or worries, only a sense of wellbeing. I am floating now, floating higher and higher, past a field of wildflowers, and under a giant rainbow, and the light is changing, changing into circular blobs, into an unidentifiable kind of bubbling energy, and then I begin to see life forms, an eye, a pair of eyes, and, and, there waiting before me is the feeling of a person. I can't quite make out who it is, but the energy feels very familiar, and loving, comforting, a strong connection, a very strong connection, like something more gentle, more primal, more pure, more something, somehow, from the past, the present and the future simultaneously. His face comes into focus, each feature more pronounced, until I see for sure that it is Arthur. Arthur, I should've known, Arthur! He's been waiting for me all along! He spins me around in his force field; a tornado of indigo light envelops us, until we separate into two entities again. I feel whole somehow. Rebalanced.

"Do you feel better now, darling?" Arthur asks me.

"So much better," I respond.

"I'm here, as your guide, to take you to the Upper World."

"Arthur? Is it you? Is it really you?"

"In the Spirit World, where you are now, dear, my name is Azure, but yes, it is me."

"I'm not going back to Earth again, am I?"

"Not now. There's a lot to consider and understand first before you return. Come with me. We are going to the Society of Elders. To talk about your life. To talk about what you learned during your most recent life, how you lived, and what you want to learn moving forward."

Together we zoom into a more open, brighter, yellowed space, and enter a wall-less classroom of sorts. There are desks and chairs, just like in my schoolroom in Redstone, but suspended in space, with nothing to hold them up, nothing to push them down either. "There's nothing to fear here, only to understand," Azure reassures me.

And it is true, more true than anything I've known before. There is nothing scary here, nothing judgmental, nothing punitive, nothing hateful, nothing but relief and peace. And wisdom.

Part 3: Redstone Boulevard

22

*M*anu was last to meet with the medium Chipeta. He didn't take much prodding, not after he had witnessed Alma and Cleve's passing over. This time, however, Chipeta made a general blessing, with her array of colored candles and incense, over the town of Redstone and the former town of Coal Basin, over all the lost souls there. She informed them that Mr. and Mrs. Osgood had finally moved on, and if they were staying behind because of them, it was time to move on now. Manu found his light, and felt a large lifting all around him. He hoped for Alma, too, but also his family, especially his mother and father, whom he loved immensely. Compared to Alma and Cleve, Manu had a big circle of family and friends who cared deeply for him during this past lifetime.

It was a mass departure that filled the library and living room with a sudden burst of light that shook the chandeliers, forcing the bulbs to flicker for a solid minute.

Rose and Kenai felt lighter, too, and Patricia exhaled so loudly the others could hear her breath emerge from deep inside her. Chipeta stood up from the floor, one movement at a time, her long limbs and layered skirt of brown, mustard-seed yellow and crimson unraveling below her. Rose, Kenai, Patricia and Chipeta all exited the castle in silence.

Outside, the sun shone brightly in a cloudless, blue sky, as sharp, freezing winds wiped their red faces. It had turned into one of the coldest afternoons of the year even though it was springtime. They said their pleasant goodbyes, pulling their coats snuggly around their bodies.

Patricia turned back into the castle; Chipeta hugged Rose and Kenai, and then retreated into her beat-up green station wagon; Rose and Kenai walked back into town, holding hands, still at a loss for words. They could feel something was missing, but also that something new would take its place. The physical plane would find an immediate way to fill the vacuum.

By the time Rose and Kenai reached town, the wind had died down and the air had warmed up, warm enough for snow to fall.

They went to their respective homes and grabbed their ice skates, reconnecting in front of the General Store. They rested for a moment surrounded by cheerful magpies. Kenai spotted one man limping heavy-footed down the street, apparently talking to a similarly dressed man amid coughing spells. Their faces and hair were coal black, and the disabled man was also missing a hand, or a whole arm, it was difficult to tell. His body continued to convulse as if he were trying to catch his breath. The men both failed to notice the snow dumping down straight through them and their filthy overcoats.

"Do you see those guys?" Kenai pointed ahead of them, questioning Rose.

"What guys?" she asked, seeing no one.

"Oh, never mind," Kenai replied. "Never mind." The syllables chee-lee-bear-a came to him. Then the repeated phrase: free us, free us, free us. But it was too much for Kenai to absorb today. He would have to let that clairauditory message go for now.

They stood up and headed for the make-shift rink down the road, passing a lone elk along the way. This particular spring season remained cold enough to contain the ice. When it wasn't freezing, there was just a small patch of dry grass and a bench, easy enough to walk right past. But in the winter, it was transformed into a place to play on ice for as long as you could stand the chill. Sometimes they'd pull out communal hockey sticks and a puck from the small, warming hut beside the rink, but today they just skated, twirling, gliding, even jumping, until they couldn't feel their cheeks anymore. They eventually made their way to Kenai's house for an ample mug of steaming, hot chocolate.

As soon as they walked through the front door, the snow began to fall, fall, fall, in silent clumps, piling up on the streets, the roof, the cars, dumping, dumping down, eerily silent but beating loudly in their full hearts, inches turning into feet. They sat by the bay window on the plaid bench covers and together observed the white mounds grow and the brave cars pass by. Their prayers for a school snow day and a powder day on the ski mountain tomorrow came true right before their very eyes.

23

*T*he film crew left the castle almost as swiftly as it had arrived. They wrapped up their three scenes as soon as Chipeta left town, one day after the clearing. Jack instantly detected the disappearance when he reentered the castle, and Chris was thrilled to continue shooting the movie, his schedule off by just a few days.

Then soon enough, one of the coldest winters on record melted into a warm, muddy spring by the end of April. The rockslides, pushing red clay from the top of the cliffs, obstructed the road on many days. There was no way to prevent the slides for the most part; a quick and tidy clean-up was the best engineering the transportation department could accomplish without moving the mountain entirely. In the most vulnerable spots, the engineers draped mesh blankets over the mountainside to contain the falling rocks.

However, there was one more mystery for Rose and Kenai to solve. What was Lady Bountiful burying by the river? They were still curious, or maybe even more so since the spirits had all departed.

When the ground finally thawed, but before the grasslands and flowers returned, the children took their chances and searched the riverbank below the castle's sloped front lawn. Rose brought one of her dad's metal detectors. As they scoured the land, they came upon a perfectly square piece of white marble a few feet from the water's edge. There were many pieces of marble along the river so that this piece didn't look too much out of place, except that it was a perfect shape, and perfectly aligned with the river, as if it had been placed there purposely by someone. The children knelt down and moved the thick stone, brushing away a top layer of softened dirt. Underneath revealed a storage box, made of pure silver.

It took many tries, and much grunting, to finally pull the box out from the ground, as it had been solidly entrenched after many years of dormancy. There wasn't any kind of lock or latch on the box; it opened quite freely. Inside were a series of red-tine bound papers, letters maybe. The words were still legible.

Kenai suggested they take the box to a warm, safe place before reading the documents. With Cleve's third wife Lucille's having burned the remainder of his papers after his death, these letters could be some of the very rare written documents left from that time. Kenai methodically lifted the heavy box and placed it bottom-down in his canvas backpack. He zipped his pack and set it on his back just as carefully.

As Rose and Kenai walked back to town, they role-played: Kenai as Cleve and Rose as Alma. Imagining themselves like bickering royalty newly arrived in the Upper World, they amused each other almost the whole trip back to town.

"You know, you look more beautiful now that you're dead than when you were alive. How is that even possible?" Kenai, pretending to be Cleve, joked.

"And you're much sweeter," Rose, pretending to be Alma, joked in return. "Which is even stranger."

"Now I'm a stranger?" Kenai acted in kind.

"No, that's not what I said. I said it was strange that you're nice now," Rose said, keeping the silly game afloat.

"But you find me strange?" Kenai said.

"Oh, forget it, you'll never understand me! Not in life or death!" Rose replied, raising her voice and pushing her hands against her wide hips. Kenai lost his composure, doubled over in laughter. Rose followed along, until they were both in tears from their happy hysterics.

Traversing the castle's front lawn, Rose tripped on an anthill. It was a large brown mound covered with sticks and weeds and numerous holes where the ants scurried in and out. When Rose hit the ground and scraped her knee, she discovered the ants. Kenai bent down beside her, his backpack still firmly set behind him. They stared at the tiny creatures fulfilling their missions. Rose reached for a skinny tree branch and pointed it towards one of the deeper holes. She deliberately inched the branch forward and placed it at the tip of the hole. A couple of ants ventured onto the branch, headed for her fingers. She lifted the branch in front of her face and studied the curious black insects. Kenai moved in closer to observe them, too, then turned his attention towards Rose's skinned knee. She caught his attention, and smiled to let him know she was okay. They returned to their study of the anthill, frozen for an elongated amount of time neither one would dare measure.

Suddenly feeling ticklish, Kenai jerked his body then brushed his ankle with his empty hand, stood up, and kicked his leg out. The ants had invaded his sneaker. Rose kicked her own leg out as well. She brushed the dirt off her knee and straightened her back.

They continued their walk back to town, never uttering another word. The warm feeling between them felt too good to disrupt.

Once they arrived safely in Kenai's green room, successfully avoiding any grown-up interference, they sat on the floor among his musical instruments and Lego creations, gingerly handling the historical papers. There were what seemed like hundreds of letters, letters to Santa Claus, written by elementary school-aged kids. They were obviously letters that Lady Bountiful had collected before her winter travels to New York and Chicago to buy Christmas gifts for the children of Redstone.

"I love that she didn't throw away or burn these letters," Rose said.

"I know," Kenai agreed. "It makes perfect sense that she wouldn't want to get rid of them, you know, because they're supposed to be at the North Pole. And she also wouldn't want anyone to find them."

"I wouldn't expect anything less from her, would you?" Rose asked.

"No, I would've done the same exact thing," Kenai asserted.

Together they removed each crinkly letter delicately, making sure not to damage them in any way. At the very bottom of the thick pile was an undated letter. It was folded in half. Rose opened it in slow motion, then read it aloud to Kenai:

Dear Ms. Shelgrem,

Hej. Var så god. It was a pleasure to meet you, as the saying goes. I have just learned about one of your country's modern treasures, August Strindberg. Are you familiar with his work? I spent some time in London among theatre people and they spoke of Strindberg's apparent genius (he is also quite popular in France now, as is Ibsen, the playwright from Norway), but that there were no English translations of Strindberg's work in circulation. Do you know of any, or perhaps be interested in some translating yourself? Outside of London, New York is the epicenter of theatre and I would delight in working to bring a production of your compatriot here.

I look forward to your affirmative response, and meanwhile send my very best wishes to you and your family.

Yours Truly,
Arthur E. Cobb

The secrecy of the note inspired Rose and Kenai to immediately return the letters to the silver box.

"I wonder if Cleve ever saw this," Kenai said, practically accusing Rose, still in his role-playing mode.

"I'm sure not. That's probably why she hid it so well, so he wouldn't," Rose answered.

"I kind of feel bad for Cleve, you know."

"You do? Why? He wasn't a very nice guy."

"But he loved her," Kenai explained.

"But not really," Rose replied.

"I don't know. That's hard to judge. How much someone loves someone else."

"Perhaps," Rose said, looking away from Kenai. "But what matters most, I think, is how you treat someone, not how much you think you love them. Because if you really loved them, you'd treat them well."

"So how about your parents? They love each other, don't they? Even if they're not always so nice to each other," Kenai said.

"I guess. It's complicated. I guess I'm just not convinced they love each other. They just think they do, for whatever reason."

"For you, Rose, you're the reason. They love each other because of you," Kenai explained.

The two of them sat together quietly for a moment. Rose began leafing through the letters again. After about a minute, Kenai gently took them from her, setting them back in the box. He offered to keep the box in his room, since it seemed to both of them safer in his room than hers. Should they turn the letters over to the Redstone Historical Society? To Patricia? Not right away, they agreed. They wanted to keep the amazing secret to themselves, at least for a while. It wasn't lying or stealing, really, they figured. There must be some kind of statute of limitations on secrets that have been hidden for over one hundred years already.

24

*I*t was June, and the rivers and creeks rushed so fast and so high that the fear of flooding captured the imagination of the entire community. For the first time in several years, though, the shops on the Boulevard were busy, and busier every day, weeks before the unofficial kick-off of summer with the Fourth of July parade. The Inn and motels were almost fully booked already, and there were more and more people on the hiking and biking trails. The people of Redstone, who unofficially convened at the Redstone General Store not only for their last-minute goods and ice cream but for gossip and local news, spoke of plentiful construction projects in the valley. Real estate brokers were showing and selling properties again. Massive logging, oil and gas trucks cruised the highway, while other industrial trucks repaved the roads with offensive tar and unwelcomed traffic. Something was definitely different, but none of them could quite explain it. Yes, the recession seemed to be ending, but then there would be another report on the radio or TV about a swift economic downturn to frighten the public. And yet, Redstone seemed completely unaffected by any such instability this summer.

On the longest day of the year, the Summer Solstice, Rose's dad's truck pulled up into their driveway. Rose had been sitting on her stoop for most of the day, drawing and reading. Every so often she'd stretch her legs and go for a short walk, but she didn't want to miss seeing her dad as soon as he arrived. He had come back to visit many times throughout the past year, but now the plan was for him to stay home for good.

When Joe stepped out of his truck wearing hole-less jeans and an un-buttoned red and black flannel shirt over his clean white T-shirt, he opened his arms wide for Rose to run straight into. It was more like sprinting. They grabbed hold of each other for an extended couple of minutes when Susie pulled her car into the driveway, just back from her job at a dentist's office in Carbondale.

Joe and Susie walked toward each other deliberately. They hugged loosely, and let go loosely, but it was a hug nonetheless.

"How was your drive?" Susie asked Joe.

"Fine," he answered. "Long."

"I can imagine," she said with empathy in her voice. "Remember that drive back east we took when I was pregnant with Rose?"

"How could I forget?" he said, smiling.

"Can I help you with your bags?" Susie asked.

"No, I'm okay. I'll get them later. I'm hungry, though. Got any food?"

"I just picked up some Chinese for us," Susie said. "Go inside, shower up if you'd like, and I'll set it all up." Susie walked back to the car and pulled out her reusable canvas grocery bag filled with take-out containers then quickly turned to Rose, who was already on the porch heading into the house.

"Hey Rosie?" her mom shouted to her.

"Yeah, mom," Rosie responded, not turning around.

"How was your day?" Susie asked.

Rose swiveled her body slightly and shouted back at her mom, "Fine," then followed her dad inside, not wanting to disrupt her mom's good mood. Joe took a lengthy, hot shower while Rose set the table and Susie changed into more comfortable clothes. Dinner was very pleasant with Rose doing most of the talking, about the end of school and what she was looking forward to this summer.

Over the next several weeks she hardly heard her parents argue. When her dad was about to get mad, about to raise his voice, he'd retreat into the bedroom or go for a walk. Her mom was eating a little healthier and hiking during her time off. She even stopped smoking. Her dad had landed a secure job as a manager for the local reclaimed lumberyard, where the owners seemed to respect and appreciate his work. Her mom got a small raise at her job pretty quickly, too.

Susie and Joe still weren't laughing that much together, but there was peace, and Rose did everything she could not to mess with it. She had gotten pretty used to thinking about them apart, visualizing a new life with the possibility of a brother or sister, but it still felt nice, however unsettling, to be under one roof again, especially without all the drama.

Her dad stopped pestering her about Kenai and actually began to like him. Rose's mom adopted a tabby cat from the animal shelter, even though her dad was allergic. It was the only solution she could find to scare away the field mice once she had discovered one too many in the trash can or darting across the wood floors when the mice thought no one was looking. The field mice were much cuter than Susie had ever expected with their petite facial features and pink ears; she didn't have the heart to trap or kill them. The cat, Zion, was a sweet and affectionate addition to the family, except for the disappointment that Mechau went missing once she arrived.

One night when Rose had her door cracked open and her parents thought she was asleep, Rose overheard them talking.

"I just feel like I had given up, you know, like I wasn't even trying, and I thought, soaking in that old hot tub for so many hours at the back of my parents' house one night, that our marriage was worth fighting for. I guess I thought I had been fighting for it, but I was really fighting against you," Joe said. "Or fighting against myself."

"Or both," Susie added. "I was in the same place as you, and now everything feels different, and I can't really explain why," Susie said.

"I know what you mean, but I don't want to question it too much. Maybe we can just enjoy it, enjoy each other, without asking questions, at least for now?"

"Okay," Susie said. "But I feel like, like, there's so much I want to say, and sometimes it's hard for me to talk to you about that kind of stuff."

"I'm trying, Susie, I am. I have so much in my mind, too, but

I just don't know how to get it out in a good way. It always comes out wrong somehow. You know, I was thinking, soon my health insurance from the job will kick in, and maybe I should start talking to someone about these kinds of things? What do you think?"

"You mean, someone professional?"

"Yeah," he responded, in almost a whisper.

"I think it's a great idea, I really do." Susie said, praising him.

"I do, too," Joe said.

"I think there are some good programs for veterans in the valley," she said. "You always said you wanted to take advantage of at least one of them."

"I know, I will. I promise…you know I've never seen you look better, or happier. Seriously. Maybe I should go away more often?" he said, half-joking.

The room went quiet, and Rose heard some moving around. She carefully closed her door because she didn't want to listen anymore. She'd heard enough. But it made her feel warm inside, hearing her parents' being so nice to one another; it gave her a sense of hope even more powerful than witnessing the spirits' disappearance into the tunneled light.

Once having Rose's dad back home became more routine, Rose and Kenai decided to explore Coal Basin. Their parents felt they were old enough now to cross the highway, although they had to bring whistles and mace with them just in case they ran into a mountain lion. Mountain lions roamed Coal Basin freely with its remote and open territory.

The children hadn't communicated with any spirits since Cleve, Alma and Manu's passing. They thought maybe their roles as spirit healers were over and done with; they were actually content to feel like regular kids for the first time in their lives.

Heading for the bridge on their bikes to the highway, they ran into Patricia who was jogging with a well-trained Alaskan Malamute dog in the opposite direction. She greeted them with a wave and a "Hello, kids." Her face looked altered somehow, uplifted. Maybe it was her facial expression, but there was something lost in the translation, as if a part of her soul had disappeared and was replaced with something lighter. It wasn't anything the children had time to discuss with one another at that moment, but they both sensed the subtle transformation.

They crossed over the highway without incident and darted past the restored beehive ovens, where they had once played hide-and-seek, then made their way up the road to Coal Basin. During the second mile, they spotted a black-faced yellow-bodied marmot digging a burrow. When the marmot spotted them, he paused and stood up on his hind legs, his front legs perched on his chest like arms, and watched them ride past.

As they approached the end of the old road's dirt section, a soft breeze wafted by them, and the clear sky gathered streaks of thin clouds. They both stopped short on their bikes when an overpowering stillness engulfed them. They turned their heads to the creek, which was trickling downstream on its way to meet up with the Crystal River off of Highway 133.

Before them, standing fully upright, a slender man was bowing his head in prayer. A Ute Native American, no doubt. The Utes once ruled this area, until they were forced out or murdered by white men, only a few decades before Cleve's arrival.

The spirit looked up suddenly, realizing that he was now known. He didn't move. The children didn't move either. They instinctively accepted that there was more serious work for them to do; they understood it was their fated duty to help this lost spirit somehow. Their short hiatus had just ended, and their next mission was now beginning.

There was no doubt for Rose at that very moment what her calling was; she wasn't going to be the most popular girl in school or a star in Hollywood. She wasn't a star at all actually, and it didn't bother her a bit. She was a vessel and a healer, and she didn't care if anyone but she and Kenai knew it. She had a best friend, and she had a purpose that would take all her very special talents to help as many spirits as she possibly could, as many spirits that would choose her to free them from the Middle World.

A crispy golden aspen leaf in the shape of a heart floated down from its ivory-hued bough to the gravely dirt road below. The fresh aroma of autumn carried with it a sense of endless possibilities, like the smell of sharpened pencils and untouched notebooks at the start of a new school year.

Clutching the grooved handlebars, the bike leaning against her muscular right thigh, Rose asked the Native American spirit matter-of-factly, "So, what's your story?"

REFERENCES

Andrews, T. (2008). *Killing for coal: America's deadliest labor war.* Cambridge, MA: Harvard University Press.

Camp & Plant (1901). Volume 1, No. 1, Cover page.

Eliot, George. (1876). *Daniel Deronda.* Edinburgh and London: William Blackwood and Sons.

Munsell, F.D. (2011). *From Redstone to Ludlow: John Cleveland Osgood's struggle against the United Mine Workers of America (Mining the American West).* Boulder, CO: University Press of Colorado.

Nelson, J. (2005). *Marble & Redstone: A quick history.* Blue Chicken, Inc.

Newton, M. (2009). *Destiny of Souls: New case studies of life between lives.* Woodbury, MN: Llewellyn Publications.

Newton, M. (1994). *Journey of Souls: Case studies of life between lives.* Woodbury, MN: Llewellyn Publications.

Pfaffmann, G., & Forsyth, H. (2008). *Rocky Mountain birds.* Woody Creek, CO: People's Press.

Pfaffmann, G., & Forsyth, H. (2007). *Rocky Mountain plants.* Basalt, CO: Bearbop Press.

Pfaffmann, G., & Forsyth, H. (2006). *Rocky Mountain mammals.* Basalt, CO: Bearbop Press.

Guided tour of the Redstone Castle by Sue McEvoy on July 3, 2014.

ACKNOWLEDGMENTS

My heart is full of grace and appreciation from - and for - all of you who have encouraged and contributed to this story and this book.

For my early readers...

Judy Appel, Andrea Barzvi, Danielle Beinstein, Tasha Blaine, Gretchen Brogdon, Cécile and Adrian Fielder, Aimee Sheeber Knight, Lily Kraft, Jane and Darrell Munsell, and Heather Wilson...

For my funders, most of whom contributed through the Kickstarter.com campaign...

Brigitte Abplanalp, Hilary Appel, Élan Barish, Bill Beer, Danielle Beinstein, Alicia Benesh, Lisa Bernard and Matt Rosenberg, Asha Veal Brisebois, Gretchen Brogdon, Karen Brogdon, Michael Brown, Pablo Caló, Rebecca Castonguay, Lori Chajet, Jay Cohen and Sheila Leunig, Janine Apter Cuthbertson, Danika Davis, Rajiv Dev, Wendy Greenberg Doucette, Jake Doucette and Remy Doucette, Lauren Enberg, Lynn Engel, Rosine and Norman Ferber, Cécile Fielder, Whitney Foley, Alesha Frederick, Gwen Garcelon, Denise Goldfarb, Hanya Gottardo, Dr. Richard Grazi, Ken Grouf and Jenny Lorant Grouf, Eric Hassman, Sara Hebert, Juliane Heyman, Brigitte Hilberman, Fiona Hoey, Sophia Kercher, Louis Kim, Aimee Sheeber Knight, Basil Kromelow, Jennifer LaTourette, Doug Levitt, Pretha Mani, Dave Mayer, Rachel and Gabe Molnar, Colleen Morrissey, Alyssa Ohnmacht, Carolyn Oswald, Janet Rasher, The Rileys, Daniel

Rosenberg, Jennifer Shaw, Bonnie Sherwood, Ann Smock, Randy and Juliet Spurrier, Glenda Summers, Anne Van Druten, Susan Vincent, and Alen Yen...

with a very special thank you to...
George Stranahan, Samantha Beinstein, Jerry and Leslie Beinstein, and Judy Appel...

For my creative team...
Robert Borviz (via 99designs.com), Gretchen Brogdon, Dana Cayton, Brittany Kohari, Larry Good, Jen Moss, Rochelle Norwood, and Alyssa Ohnmacht...

For my 2015-6 middle school students, this story's first audience...
Ava, Becca, Celeste, Colton, Erica, Grace, Kaley, Kosara, Maddiy, Orangie, Tomas, Wyatt and Xavier...

...may your homes always be blessed with peace and loving kindness, and your souls free to fulfill their purpose.

Photo credit: Danielle Beinstein

ABOUT THE AUTHOR

Nicole Beinstein has loved to write ever since she was a young girl growing up in Hong Kong and New York City. She studied psychology at Cornell University and then business at the Yale School of Management, where she was chosen as her class' commencement speaker. As a grown-up, she has held many different kinds of jobs in multiple industries, which have all provided her with great experiences, knowledge and stories for her writing. She won three book awards in 2010 for a photographic memoir that she co-authored with George Stranahan, and is currently teaching middle school at a rural charter school as well as Sustainable Business at Colorado Mountain College in the Colorado Rocky Mountains. She moved to Redstone, Colorado with her family in 2007.

Made in the USA
Middletown, DE
25 June 2016